When the introductions began, Mary could hardly believe it. She was to meet Major-General Charles O'Hara, who had just arrived from Rome.

O'Hara!

The sound of that name affected her in a very odd way.

O'Hara's face was one she would never forget, even though she saw it through a blur, for the very mention of his name brought back that evening at Lord Cowper's party so forcefully that she almost felt faint. That dimly lighted room, the shock of that awful revelation, her despairing sob and the sudden emergence of her comforter from the shadows—the stranger passing by—Charles O'Hara!

Now they were face to face under the blazing chandeliers. His bow was courtly, his greeting formal and correct. Here was the man Mary thought she would never see again—and now that he was with her at last he acted as if he didn't remember her at all!

A Heart Denied

(Original title: *Caste for Comedy*)

Audrey Curling

ace books

A Division of Charter Communications Inc.
A GROSSET & DUNLAP COMPANY
360 Park Avenue South
New York, New York 10010

A HEART DENIED

(Original title: *Caste for Comedy*)

Copyright © 1970 by Audrey Curling

An ACE Book by arrangement with
Hurst & Blackett Ltd.

Printed in U.S.A.

A HEART DENIED

1

THE COLD OF the marble balustrade struck into Mary's hand and shattered the illusion of unreality she had felt all the evening. The grand double staircase sweeping proudly up under the magnificent painted ceiling of Lord Cowper's house was substantial under her feet. There was no doubt of its reality— or of hers.

She was Mary Berry from London and with her father and her sister, Agnes, she had been welcomed into the circle that rotated round Lord and Lady Cowper in Florence with an alacrity that compensated her for some of the slights she had suffered at home.

They had spent several enchanted weeks in the city and Lady Cowper's pretty young sister, Emily Gore, an enthusiastic guide, had shown Mary most of the sights and been rewarded by her appreciation. Miss Gore's unaffected friendliness soon dispelled the shyness that masked Mary's lack of confidence.

Now, as a culminating diversion, they were attending one of Lord Cowper's fabulous receptions which they had heard so much about but never expected to see.

"What a lucky thing it was meeting some influential travelling gentlemen on the way," Mary thought. "If I hadn't screwed up courage to ask one of them for a letter of introduction we certainly wouldn't be here!"

But, as a result of her initiative, she was following Miss Gore up a staircase such as she had only seen in paintings to fetch the letters that would introduce them into the most exclusive circles in Rome.

"I insist you shall meet *everyone*," Miss Gore had declared when she heard they were leaving for Rome in a day or so and she had set about writing the first letter with Mary at her elbow scarcely daring to breathe as she saw the magic words "Florence, December 12th, 1783," appear on the paper.

"I finished my last letter as the guests began to arrive," Miss Gore said as they went up. "Oh me, I wish I could come with you. Do you know I never yet met a father who has devoted himself so entirely to his daughters as yours has done? I can't think how he has escaped matrimony for he's so easy and good-humoured. Mr. Berry must be a most remarkable man."

2

"Yes, I rather think he is," Mary assented, and a smile with just a hint of amusement in it lit up her face. Pa was undoubtedly remarkable in some ways but as Miss Gore was not likely to notice more than his charm of manner, his delight in literary pursuits and his affability in pleasant society she felt sure his less admirable traits would remain undiscovered.

"No," Mary thought, "there's no need to divulge our family history to Miss Gore or to anybody else and I don't want to think of it myself if I can help it."

Her life—her real life—had begun with their travels and her delight in seeing dear Pa so happy and carefree now that they were financially better off outweighed the twinges of resentment she felt because he left all the arrangements for their prolonged tour to her. So long as nobody suspected that it was she who did all the haggling and bargaining with innkeepers and voituriers what did it matter?

She had soon found out how to beat landlords down. She simply repeated the price she thought fair in a loud and resolute voice until she got her way. She had dealt with other contingencies, too. When poor Pa grew nervous at Bologna because he'd heard travellers were being murdered for their money she marched straight into an awful little shop, her heart pounding with sheer terror but her chin held high, and demanded a stiletto.

She didn't get one because the shopkeeper told her it was against the law to sell them but at least she had made the effort and calmed her father with the information. "And I don't suppose Miss Gore ever did such a thing," she thought. "She'd have had a retinue of servants, but I learned a great deal of Italian in the process and here we are after all our adventures and with even better things to come."

And because she was so excited she couldn't help exclaiming aloud:

"This is a dream come true! I've been thinking of Italy ever since Mr. Zoffany painted our portrait and talked our ears off about it and about Florence and Lord and Lady Cowper, too."

"And you're not disappointed?"

"How could I be? Everything's better than he led me to expect. He can't paint in words, you know!"

"Just wait till you see Rome. You'll find it even more exciting, I think."

They had reached a corridor with doors on each side. Suddenly Miss Gore stopped by one of them, put her finger to her lips and said rather impishly: "Would you like a treat? I'm going to show you the musicians' gallery."

She opened a door leading to a balcony from which they could look down on the drawing room which was beginning to fill with guests.

"I love watching everyone drift in after supper—some of them look so different viewed from above," she said. "Lord Cowper says I'm very naughty to peep but I can't resist it sometimes. And, you know, people are so absorbed in themselves they scarcely ever look up unless the musicians are here."

"Oh, it's beautiful!" Mary exclaimed.

The cold marble floor of the vast drawing room was richly carpeted and a great log fire blazed at either end. Three chandeliers winked and glittered and flashed with the brilliance of clustering diamonds, but Mary was even more dazzled by the women's clothes. Such a collection of gleaming satins, iridescent taffetas, glowing silks and voluptuous velvets had never been gathered together before, she thought.

And everyone was talking. She was fascinated by the sound of voices. They were sweet, tender, mocking, insinuating; they were low, shrill, harsh, melodious. An exclamation would make a sudden puncturing stab, laughter rippled, snorted, exploded and erupted in parrot-like squeals.

"How intriguing to hear so many different tongues spoken at once!" she exclaimed. "French, German, English, Italian. Oh, how I long to know Italian thoroughly."

"When you are in Rome go to Signor Dalmazzoni for lessons," Miss Gore advised. "I'll give you his address."

"You're so kind to me," Mary said impulsively.

Miss Gore smiled. "My dear Miss Berry, is that such a surprise? I can't imagine anybody not being kind to you."

Mary said—"It's wonderful—it's all so wonderful," and then she caught sight of her sister below and said: "Oh, look! There's Agnes!"

After watching for a moment she added softly: "I never look at her without wishing her mother could see her! Look, she's talking to Sir Horace Mann."

"My dear, he is talking to her. And if I know

anything he's asking her what she thinks of Strawberry Hill and enquiring what improvements had been made there lately quite forgetting he asked her the same thing only yesterday. He thinks everyone in England has been to Strawberry Hill," said Miss Gore.

"Is it a dreadful confession to say we haven't seen it although we lived quite close to Twickenham for years?" Mary asked. "And we don't know its owner either. I doubt if we shall ever meet Mr. Walpole but I'm growing ashamed of my ignorance for everyone in Florence seems to have some tale of him. To know nothing of him at all makes people think one quite odd!"

"Then I'm odd too, for I don't know him either," said Miss Gore. "And why should I?—or you, for that matter? He's not of our time, my dear. Why, he must be older than Methuselah! He came to Italy in 1740 and that's over forty years ago!"

"And yet he's still remembered here?"

"Because he struck up a friendship with Sir Horace Mann and they've corresponded ever since though they've never met again! Don't you think it odd?"

"Whatever do they find to say?" asked Mary.

"Oh, everything—politics and fashion and gossip and scandal. And Strawberry Hill, of course. Mr. Walpole has devoted years to that odd house of his and it's something more than a child to him now. I think it's rather dreadful."

"Why?" asked Mary.

"Because a man should marry and have children and all Mr. Walpole has is a lot of stained glass. For heaven's sake, don't tell anyone I said so!"

"You may depend on me," Mary said.

"And of course, being who he is, the son of Sir Robert Walpole, he knows everyone and many people think that to be a friend of Mr. Walpole is to be made in the eyes of the world," Miss Gore went on.

"Then I'm afraid the Berrys must remain unmade," Mary laughed. "Italy is far more exciting than Twickenham could ever be!"

"I'm sure you're right and I've so much more to show you yet," said Miss Gore, "but I'll fetch the letters now or we shall be missed. Would you like to wait for me here?"

"Oh yes. The scene's enchanting," Mary said.

She wished she could scoop it up whole and keep it intact. "How thrilled dear Grandmother Seton will be when I write of all this," Mary thought when she was alone. "She never believed we'd come to Italy at all. And neither we would if I hadn't coaxed and persuaded and planned till my head was ready to split. But here we are and we're going to enjoy every second of it and if she only knew that Agnes was strolling round the room with Sir Horace Mann whatever would she think?"

Agnes appeared to be listening to the Ambassador with rapt attention and Mary was surprised to find that she, too, could hear what he was saying without any effort.

"Have you seen any of these new-fangled balloons that are all the rage in France, Miss Agnes?" he asked.

"Not yet, Sir Horace. But *do* tell me about them," Agnes said.

"Men go up in the air in them! I had it from Mr. Walpole who has no doubt at all that we shall soon reach the moon and reduce it to a province of Europe! What do you say to that?"

"I'd say it's a delightful flight of fancy," Agnes replied. "Does he indulge in them much?"

They passed on before Mary could hear the reply but she could see Sir Horace was well away. Then she found she could distinguish other English voices with remarkable ease.

On a sofa just beneath the gallery sat Mrs. Tristram who had lived in Florence for years passing the time by tearing characters to shreds. She gleaned scraps of gossip from the capitals of Europe and travellers were often horrified to find that their less creditable adventures were already known in Florence when they arrived.

Mrs. Tristram had been affable to the Berrys and seeing that she was obviously speaking of Agnes to her friend Miss Mayhew, Mary couldn't resist the temptation to listen.

The voices came up piercingly clear for Mrs. Tristram's had the quality of a post-horn and Miss Mayhew possessed its rival.

"You must admit she's handsome," Miss Mayhew trumpeted, as though there might be some argument about it. "How old would you say?"

"About nineteen, I suppose. An ingratiating young person. Just see how she's drawing the Ambassador out," said Mrs. Tristram. Her tone surprised Mary for she had expected to hear a compliment.

She stayed very still.

Miss Mayhew leaned towards Mrs. Tristram and asked in an inquisitive voice:

"Who *are* the Berrys? Do you know anything of them?"

"Only that the father was disinherited. I had it from my nephew, Mr. Gilbert. It's a very strange story but there's no doubt that Mr. Berry had expectations of enormous wealth and was cut off."

"Heavens above! What does he live on?" asked Miss Mayhew.

"On the charity of his brother, my dear. He has a mere pittance of his own but there's nothing for his daughters. And there won't be, either."

"I wonder what he did to merit such a fate? Those girls will be hard put to it to get husbands if he can't give them a dowry," Miss Mayhew announced.

The words struck Mary like arrows robbing her of voice and movement. She was no longer listening—she was being forced to hear.

"Wouldn't you expect people in their position to stay at home and practise economy?" Mrs. Tristram said. "I suspect they've only come abroad in the hope of trapping a rich t.g. who won't have heard their story. What else could it be?"

"I notice Miss Gore has taken them up," observed Miss Mayhew.

"Oh yes. They've made a good impression there I grant you, and the elder Miss Berry has worked hard for it."

She tapped Miss Mayhew on the arm with her fan and said significantly, "She means to have a place. In spite of her pretty face and simple ways that young lady is a designing woman if ever I saw one."

"Well, you've intrigued me vastly," said Miss Mayhew. "I must have a closer look at her and I don't see her this evening."

"Nor do I. I wonder where she can be?" said Mrs. Tristram.

A sense of outrage and indignation such as she had seldom felt before took possession of Mary at that moment. It was frightening but uncontrollable. She leaned over the balcony and said coldly:

"I am here, Mrs. Tristram."

"Heavens!" exclaimed Mrs. Tristram, starting from her seat. "What a fright you gave me, Miss Berry."

"Some of your facts are right, Mrs. Tristram, but your assumptions spring from fancy, I suppose. However, I don't feel obliged to put you right on that score."

"Why, I declare you're laughing at us both!" tittered Miss Mayhew nervously. "I believe you're quizzing us. Have you been up there long?"

"Long enough to learn that what I've often been told is true. Listeners hear no good of themselves," Mary said.

She spoke in a level tone but her heart was racing. She was mortally wounded and the room which had seemed so pleasant and civilised a few minutes before had suddenly become a jungle.

A dull pain was beginning just above her right eye. It was the first warning of the nervous headaches she was subject to and she knew it would get worse.

The sounds of gaiety from below aggravated her misery and she sped down the stairs into the deserted supper room where only one lamp burned. She slammed the door, flung herself down on a sofa and let her disillusionment tear her to pieces.

Tears stung her eyes sharper than vinegar on a cut and she felt as though a volcano was seething inside her. It was as though all the slights and injustices she had borne since early childhood had gathered into a monstrous tumour that was all ready to burst and spread its poison through her veins.

She could have borne what Mrs. Tristram had said better if she had not heard it at the height of her happiness and realised the fragility of the peak she had supposed herself to be so safe on. She didn't know how she was ever to regain calm. And how was she to reassemble the weapons she needed in her fight to gain the position in society which should have been her family's by right?

She wanted a friend, somebody who would understand the disadvantages she had to contend with, but there wasn't anyone. She allowed a sob to escape. It was such an indescribable relief that another began to rise which she choked back as the sound of a chair being pushed away from the table startled her.

A man was rising from it. She could just make him out in the dim light, tall and broad and powerful, as he seized the lamp from the sideboard and held it aloft, looking round the room.

What on earth was she to do? She couldn't escape because he was between her and the door, so she cowered low in the hope he wouldn't notice her and would go away, but he had seen her and he broke into a laugh.

"Bless my soul! You woke me up!" he exclaimed.

He had a deep voice with a tone which struck her most pleasantly. The hint of a lilt and his attractive pronunciation made his manner of speech unusual and there was also a note of humourous understanding which created an instantaneous atmosphere of warmth.

"I didn't mean to wake you—I thought I was alone," she said.

"You were too occupied with whatever brought you away from the bright lights outside to notice me," he said. "I've been here an hour and was most ungracefully asleep with my head on the table after demolishing the feast Lord Cowper was so kind as to leave me with."

"You were not with the company at supper?"

"No. I was late and tired with hard riding and I was just dreaming about a rose garden and a pretty girl who was going to wake me with a kiss when the closing of a door brought me back to this villainous world again."

"I'm sorry I broke your dream—I'll leave you to finish your sleep," she said.

"No." He came towards her, a giant shadow in that room full of shadows. "It wasn't only the slam of a door. There was something else. I heard weeping."

"Please to remember I thought myself alone," she said, mustering all her dignity though she could not prevent her voice from trembling.

"I heard a heart breaking. Believe me—I know the sound! Forgive me for my flippancy when I first spoke and allow me to make amends for it. Will you permit me to help you?"

"But I don't know you and you don't know me," she protested wonderingly.

"Isn't that all the better? Strangers make better confidants than friends in rare instances—or I'm much mistaken. I am a stranger passing through this city and in a way of life that keeps me moving about the world."

He came a step closer and said: "I can see enough of you to tell you are very young, most vulnerable, and that you have been hurt damnably."

No one ever before had summed up her situation with such telling accuracy—it was as though her soul had been absorbed in his for an infinitesimal moment and given him a knowledge of her feelings that she could never have imparted in years. She was inclined to a certain alarm.

"You are frighteningly perceptive, but the hurt is nothing—except to me," she said. "It was something I overheard—idle gossip, you might call it, but as cruel and fatal to me as any I could imagine."

"Ah, but we all know how words can wound. This will be forgotten the moment another subject rises," he said compassionately.

"Not by me! What I heard was worthless and stupid enough but it served to show me how my situation appears to others and that is something I never came face to face with until tonight."

She had begun vehemently, but her voice trembled away as she finished.

"I ask no questions, but if you have suffered some misfortune, though it's through no fault of your own, you'll find spiteful tongues won't distinguish between those who inflict the evil and those who are the victims of it. Indeed, it often makes a better story when it is told against the one who suffers."

"But that's unfair!" she exclaimed hotly.

"True. I know it to my cost."

"You? I'm sorry to think that anyone should be made unhappy," she said, her voice warming with the sympathy that sprang from her special understanding. "I would help you if I could," she added impulsively.

"I believe you would indeed! But mine aren't the kind of misfortunes that can be mended and I suspect that yours are. So let us forget about mine. Nobody worth a second thought could think ill of you—I feel sure of it. Just now I called the world a villainous place. That was before we knew each other. We may never meet again but before I go on my way tell me you'll take heart. You can if you rely on yourself. Believe me."

Mary was silent as she thought of what Mrs. Tristram had said and realised the way in which the world might see her. Mrs. Tristram had attached no blame to the uncle who had cheated her father out of his fortune and blighted all his hopes—and all hers too.

How right this stranger was! She saw with a sudden and devastating clarity that she had nobody to depend upon but herself and that her father's and sister's fortunes as well as her own rested on her shoulders because she was so much stronger than either of them.

"But I don't want to be the strong one!" she cried out inside herself.

She felt as though the weight of responsibility was too much for her to take, but in the same instant she experienced a second strength prevailing—one she had not known lay within her.

She drew herself up proudly.

"I shall always try to do what is right. I can promise you that," she said.

"Then you have nothing in the world to fear."

"And I shall only do what is safe," she added a shade primly.

"Even if it isn't agreeable?"

"Oh, but I hope it will be!"

His laugh rang out. "If you keep danger at bay in the world we live in you'll make history! You have a sense of humour, I see. I wish you'd let me do something to serve you," he said.

"Then I will. Please send someone to find Miss Gore and ask her to come to me here. I have a vile headache and shall not rejoin the company tonight."

"I'm sorry for that and I'll do your bidding. Are you not glad we met?"

"Indeed I am. I shall not forget you—even though I don't know your name."

"My name is O'Hara," he said, "Charles O'Hara."

2

EMILY GORE WAS at Mary's side almost immediately.

The too-familiar symptoms, a blinding headache accompanied by distressing nausea were increasing, but Mary was anxious to avoid fuss—"I don't want to spoil the evening for Papa and Agnes so pray let me leave quietly," she pleaded.

Her longing to be away from the magnificent house was now even stronger than her previous wish to visit it.

"Sally is at Mr. Megot's and she knows so well how to nurse me—she's used to my turns," she assured Miss Gore.

Sally Oakroyd was a farmer's daughter from Kirkbridge in Yorkshire where Robert Berry and his young wife had spent their short married life. Now she was in Italy as maid to Mary and Agnes.

"Leave everything to me, my dear Miss Berry," said Miss Gore with an intuitive understanding of Mary's need. "I shall feel quite easy if you are to be in Sally's care."

The mere thought of Sally was a comfort to Mary. The girl had been her humbly devoted friend from the day they had first met as small children and though both had been aware of the difference in their stations from the first Mary had been quick to see other differences, too.

Sally had worn a bright cotton dress that day. Mary was in mourning for her mother and was making a call at the Oakroyd's farm with her grandmother. They did not go in. Mrs. Oakroyd came out to their carriage bobbing respectfully to Mrs. Seton at this mark of condescension from the quality.

In spite of this Mary was aware even then that her family was living in the chill of a cold, mean shadow, some sort of inexplicable disgrace, and she had stared in wonder at the fat, laughing little girl who was cuddling a kitten and looked so safe in the shelter of her mother's skirts.

Sally was just as much of a dumpling now as she had been then but she had grown up with good hands and she was practical, pretty and reliable.

But she was not to be found at the hotel when Mary arrived.

By that time she was so ill that she was glad to let one of the hotel maids help her into bed and as she lay in the dark the intolerable throbbing pain made thought impossible and she scarcely knew who came and went.

On the second day the pain subsided and she began to feel better. She began to think and to remember what had happened at the Cowpers' and how the world had tumbled to pieces.

She remembered Mrs. Tristram's disparaging tones and squirmed. "To assume that *I* should be deep and designing because Pa has been so unlucky!" she thought.

The whole evening came back to her—not only the episode of Mrs. Tristram but of the man in the dining room with whom she had been so uncharacteristically confidential.

O'Hara. Charles O'Hara. She had talked to him so freely! She had revealed her thoughts and feelings and resolutions almost as though she were under a spell. Who on earth could he have been?

She opened her eyes wide and saw that Sally, seated beside her bed, was looking at her with a woebegone expression.

"Oh, Miss Mary dear, I'll never forgive myself for being away when you were brought back so ill," she said. "I went off in a party with the other maids and men to see what we could of the junketings at the grand houses. There wasn't any harm at all but there was a Mr. MacCarthey who seemed to take a fancy to me and he's such a talker that somehow we got separated from the others and I never thought it could be so late."

"It's the first time you ever slipped off without asking me first," Mary said. "Still, you're forgiven. But I hope you kept him in his place."

"Oh I did, Miss Mary, and when he said he'd give a pot of gold for a taste of my Yorkshire pudding I was as sharp with him as you could wish."

"The impudence! And the gold's at the foot of the rainbow, I suppose. What's his Christian name?"

"Rory."

"Heavens above! He wouldn't be Irish, would he?" Mary laughed.

"Oh, it is good to see you so much better, Miss Mary," declared Sally. "You'll be up in no time."

"I shall be up now," Mary said, hoisting herself up rather gingerly on her pillows. "We must be getting ready to go. I haven't forgotten what day it is, Sally, even though you may have done."

As she spoke the door opened to admit Agnes who was relieved to see her sister so much recovered.

"I won't disturb you," she said. "You must take things easily for a while yet."

"No, please don't go, Agnes," Mary said. "I'm so much better I want to see the morning sky. I'm quite recovered, you see."

"You still look pale," remarked Agnes as Sally opened the shutters flooding the room with December sunlight.

"My face will glow when I've dashed it with ice-water! Will you help me to dress, for I intend to sit like a queen and supervise the packing so there'll be no delays in the morning. Sally, you may tell Mr. Berry that I'm quite myself again."

"But you're not nearly strong enough to travel

yet," protested Agnes as soon as they were alone. Pa and I both think we should stay here several days more."

"And miss being in Rome for Christmas? I should think not. It'll take a week to get there at our rate of going and the voiturier is already engaged. If we lost this chance we might have to wait weeks for mules."

"What would it matter? We're with friends! Miss Gore has sent to enquire after you several times a day and Mrs. Tristram's been most concerned, too."

Mary's laugh was derogatory. "Mrs. Tristram's concern is really too touching," she said.

Agnes looked puzzled. "She told me she feared you were sickening for something for you spoke to her in such an odd manner before you took ill," she said. "I think you hurt her feelings."

"Agnes, it's my duty to warn you that Mrs. Tristram is an old cat," responded Mary, bridling at this.

"Gracious! What makes you say that?"

"Certain knowledge. I don't think we should associate with her."

"I can hardly believe you mean it. She's as concerned about Pa being cheated out of his fortune as if our troubles were hers, and she thinks old Mr. Ferguson and our Uncle William behaved shamefully," Agnes declared.

"So she got our story from you!" exclaimed Mary. "I suppose she dragged it out of you?"

"She took an interest," Agnes said defensively. "After all, Mary, Pa's never hidden it so why should we? And what is there to be ashamed of, I'd like to know?"

"Nothing. Nothing in the world so far as we are concerned," Mary said. "But Mrs. Tristram knows what we ought to have had and she also knows what we've got. She has persuaded herself and may try to persuade others that we're looking out for cunning ways to advance ourselves."

"I can scarcely believe it!" Agnes cried.

"I heard her say so. That's evidence enough for me."

"But she has only to look at us! Are you sure you're right?" Agnes pleaded, unwilling to think ill of someone she had looked on as a friend.

"Positive."

"Very well, Mary," Agnes said after a pause. "I shall be guided by you for you always seem to know best, though it's dreadfully disconcerting."

She looked so downcast that Mary said: "Don't fret, Agnes dear. We'll both be a little more wary in future. And now do tell me how the evening at the Cowpers' ended, and what you did yesterday. I'm dying to know."

"Oh, it's all been heaven—or at least it would have been if only you'd been there," Agnes said. "There was a man at the Cowpers' who caused quite a furore. You'd have died laughing to see how all the women fluttered and preened themselves and clustered round him as though he was the cock in the barnyard."

"You weren't among them, I'll be bound," said Mary.

"Heavens, no. But I didn't lose anything for

yesterday Pa and I went to call on Sir Horace Mann and who should be there but this very gentleman and Sir Horace was treating him as though he was of the blood royal."

"And is he?"

"No, my dear. That's what makes it all so intriguing. He's a bastard."

"Heavens! Whose?"

"Someone I never even heard of but Miss Gore told me all about him for there's no secret in it. His father was a dreadful old Irish peer called Tyrawley who was a famous enough soldier in his day but a terrible rip. The women he ruined you'd never count in a month of Sundays, it's said. Yet, for all that, he was A.D.C. to our late king who made him his Ambassador to Portugal. And when he came back—oh—you'll never guess what he brought with him!"

"Sacks of gold, I suppose."

"Gracious no. Three wives and fourteen children! Can you imagine the scene at Dover?"

"And are you asking me to believe that one of this brood was nearly mobbed at the Cowpers' and specially honoured by Sir Horace? Why?"

"Because he's a hero. Yes, he really is magnificent. He's a soldier and a valiant one and he's not long returned from the war in America, but that's only one of the many he's been in."

"What's he called?"

"O'Hara," Agnes said. "Major-General Charles O'Hara, and don't forget to curtsey. Why, what's the matter?"

"Nothing," Mary said quickly. "What else do you know?"

"You'll have to ask Miss Gore for the rest," Agnes said.

As Miss Gore arrived to enquire after Mary shortly after this the sisters adjourned to their dressing room to receive her and when she was assured of Mary's recovery she said:

"Now I do hope you'll consent to stay in Florence a few days longer, my dear friends. General O'Hara's arrival has stimulated everyone! This isn't the time to run away."

Mary blinked and flicked an imaginary crumb from her dress with a lace handkerchief and said: "Oh, what a pity. I fear Papa has our plans too advanced to alter them now."

"General O'Hara's waiting here for one of the Conways to join him," Miss Gore rattled on, not noticing Mary's embarrassment. "He's a great favourite of old Marshal Conway whose nephew is to come to Italy for his health which is very poor. O'Hara will take him under his wing."

"Are not the Conways a noble family?" Mary enquired.

"Oh, indeed. And closely connected with Mr. Walpole, too. Cousins, I believe."

Mary laughed. "Who isn't connected with Mr. Walpole?" she asked.

"His net spreads over the whole of society—he's even got O'Hara in its meshes. They are well acquainted and I shouldn't wonder if he entrusted O'Hara with letters for Sir Horace. He uses all sorts of messengers. But there, I'm tiring you."

"Oh no, not at all!"

"Even so I must leave for I've so many calls to

make. Can I really not tempt you to defer your journey to Rome? My sister and Lord Cowper wish it as much as I.''

Mary was not to be persuaded so at last Miss Gore said: ''Well, my dear friends, I must bid you au revoir for the present then. I shall see you again before you go.''

They watched from the window as she drove away and as there was so much to see in the courtyard they stayed there after she had gone and Agnes fetched her sketch book and began to draw.

''I'll never do horses,'' she sighed.

Sally came in to say that Mr. Berry had not yet returned from riding and stayed to watch a fine black horse being led out of the stables. Presently a tall, powerfully built man came into the courtyard and swung into the saddle followed by a much shorter one who mounted a nag.

Mary heard Sally catch her breath sharply and was surprised to see her eyes were fixed on the small man, but Agnes diverted her attention by exclaiming excitedly:

''Why Mary, that's General O'Hara on the black horse! Do take a good look at him. If you work out all the battles he's been in he must be nearly as old as Pa, but he's a fine figure of a man, don't you think?''

''I think he must be a very fine man altogether,'' Mary said thoughtfully.

''There he goes,'' Agnes said as the General rode out of the yard.

''And there goes Rory after him,'' murmured Sally, watching the small man who rode the nag with a swagger that made Mary want to laugh. Then she suddenly realised that this was the man who had kept Sally out so late. This was the Mac-Carthey she had blushed over and now he was riding away with O'Hara whose serving man he obviously was.

At that moment Rory MacCarthey looked up at their window, waved his hand and bowed. He had a spud-grey skin and eyes like splinters of aquamarine.

Sally fluttered her handkerchief at him and Mary saw her eyes were brimming. She was touched to see the childlike innocence of her face at that moment.

O'Hara did not look back. There was no reason why he should and yet she wished she could have had a view of his face in the clear winter sunlight. It would have been a memory to treasure.

She felt sure the O'Hara who had comforted her at the Cowper's was known only to her—as perhaps she was known only to him.

3

MARY WAS DELIGHTED with their lodgings in Rome. She inspected the spacious rooms minutely when they arrived pointing out all the advantages to her father and Agnes.

"We shall be able to entertain!" she exclaimed. "Oh Pa, won't that be gratifying? Such elegant furnishings, you see!"

"All in exquisite taste," agreed Mr. Berry, his amiable face beaming at her pleasure.

"Linen and plate included too!" she went on. "At twenty sequins the month we're more than fortunate."

"How you do weigh everything up, Mary!" objected Agnes, putting down a porcelain figurine she had been admiring as though the mention of money would debase it.

"I have to, since you never do," replied Mary, feeling slightly dashed.

"But things always plan out so well I don't see why anyone need bother to keep adding up and subtracting. Do you, Pa?"

"Your sister has a practical mind, my dear, and that's to be commended. *You* are the artistic one, Agnes. We can't all be alike."

"And you are the literary one, Pa," said Agnes. "I suppose our united qualities combine rather well."

"Beautifully," agreed Mr. Berry. "Beautifully." He made the word last a long time as though it were a sweetmeat to be kept in the mouth.

Mary was half-amused and half-irritated by the way they both assumed that all the advantages she took such pains to procure happened by magic. That very morning she had scored a minor triumph by persuading Signor Dalmazzoni, who was to teach her Italian, to take Agnes as well—two for the price of one.

But Agnes would never understand how important such transactions were in the spinning out of their limited means so she didn't bother to tell her.

She easily shook off the slight feeling of pique at the thought of the wonders they were to see.

"Isn't it exciting to be in Rome!" she exclaimed. "Just wait until we find our feet and begin to explore. Did you ever think we'd arrive, Pa?"

"There were times when I wondered if we were really in Italy or in an Irish bog," Mr. Berry admitted.

The journey from Florence was one of those things you could laugh over in retrospect, Mary said. Those execrable inns, the bug-ridden beds, the imperishable fleas, the disgusting food and the discomfort of being so wet and cold had been hard to endure at times.

"No one but my dear Mary would have had the persistence to make those intractable landlords light fires for us," Mr. Berry said proudly.

"Or coughed so hard from the smoke of the wet sticks they used," she said. "The horses were much more comfortable than we were—I quite envied the beasts in their stables."

She would be able to laugh over these discomforts but she would never be able to laugh over Mrs. Tristram's heartless remarks which had troubled her ever since she had heard them. She was afraid she would never quite eradicate them from her mind and hoped they would not meet people like her in Rome.

At the illustrious houses whose doors were opened to them through Miss Gore's influence their reception was as cordial as she could have wished and soon they were paying and receiving calls, attending receptions, dinners and concerts and meeting the most sought-after of the English visitors as well as members of the Italian aristocracy and eminent church dignitaries.

Time passed so quickly that it was almost impossible to believe that Florence was already three months away, but the violets were flowering, there was the softness of spring in the air and more visitors arrived every day. They never knew who they would meet next, especially when they went to Cardinal de Bernis for he held such wonderful conversazziones—better than anybody else's, Mary thought.

"To-night's should exceed everything," Agnes said excitedly one day. "The King of Sweden and the Emperor of Germany will both be there, princes and princesses, dukes and duchesses galore, some sprigs of our own nobility and a certain Mr. Robert Berry with the two Miss Berrys! The house is to be illuminated!"

She was dancing round the room and she began to whirl her father round with her.

"I wonder who we shall meet, Pa! Isn't it exciting never to know?" she said.

"Yes, and rather frightening, too," Mary put in. "You never know when your fate will change."

Mr. Berry put his hand to his head with sudden melancholy. "That is an indisputable fact," he said, and went slowly from the room leaving the girls gazing at each other sorrowfully.

"Poor Pa! I suppose he thought of our mother and all the happiness he lost when she died," said Agnes. "Oh Mary, isn't it a blessing he has us? We'll never leave him, will we?"

Mary sighed. "He has wonderfully resilient spirits now that we live so much more comfortably," she said. "He'll soon recover."

Sally was waiting to help them dress for the evening and as Mary sat before the looking glass while the girl arranged her hair she noticed how thoughtful she seemed. She had often recalled the look on Sally's face when they watched General O'Hara and his serving man ride away from the hotel in Florence. Sally, usually so cheerful, gave a gusty sigh.

"I do hope you don't regret making this journey with us, Sally," Mary said. "You've been more than a help to me as well as a friend, but sometimes I doubt if you're happy?"

"Lawks, Miss, I'm right enough," declared Sally stoutly. "Mind, I wouldn't care to be here in any company but yours. I don't like foreign ways. And I don't care to be woken at four in the morning by all those cows and goats coming to the doors to be milked."

"And you from a farm, Sally!" laughed Mary.

"They don't bring the cattle to the front door of our farmhouse," objected Sally. "And as to that Piazza whatever they call it . . . "

"The Piazza di Spagna, Sally," said Mary.

"A very fine name for a place that's ankle deep in muck! And what's worse a lot of natives behave as natural as the animals. I often don't know which way to look!"

"But the churches and the statues and the masses of flowers, Sally! And the fountains! And the colours! And see how lovely the Trinita dei Monti looks with the sky so blue and the cypresses! You thought Florence beautiful, didn't you?"

"It wasn't Florence. It was Rory MacCarthey."

"But you scarcely know him!" exclaimed Mary in astonishment.

"Maybe not. But a person can fall in love at first sight," replied Sally stolidly.

"Not with a hard Yorkshire head like yours," remarked Mary.

"But I've a strong heart," Sally replied. "I wouldn't have left home to come here where it's so much dirtier and stinks so bad if I hadn't loved you and wanted to serve you, would I, Miss Mary? And if I loved a man I'd journey much further and be still more uncomfortable."

"Sally, I don't mean to pry, but are you seriously thinking yourself in love with Rory?" Mary asked.

"There's no thinking about it. I *am* in love with him."

"Oh, Sally, do beware. I fell in love at first sight myself once and the fever lasted exactly three weeks. Then it vanished completely and I couldn't so much as bear the sight of the poor young man afterwards."

The expression on Sally's face checked her from enlarging on this.

"That may be, but my heart tells me the truth, Miss Mary. Yours will do the same when you meet a man worth loving."

Mary shook her head. "I've learned by my first experience," she said.

"Time will tell," Sally said, as she put the finishing touches to Mary's attire. "You may not fall in love with anyone yourself yet awhile but if someone doesn't fall in love with you this very night I'm not Sally Oakroyd as longs to be Sally MacCarthey!"

Cardinal de Bernis' magnificent rooms were crowded that evening and the street outside was thronged with people staring at his illuminations and watching the distinguished guests arrive.

Mary always found the old prelate absolutely fascinating and loved to watch the way his lively expression transformed his ugly face into one she delighted to watch.

"He would be my favourite subject if I could only draw," she whispered to Agnes.

"But his face doesn't stay the same two minutes together," objected Agnes.

"That's the wonderful thing about it!"

The Cardinal had just sent a group of men round him into convulsions with one of his witty remarks when he spotted Mary and moved towards her welcoming her paternally as his "fille chérie." He conversed with her in French as he said they could meet on equal terms in that language, but she often found it hard work to keep up with his brilliant flow.

But this evening she had no difficulty in understanding what he said for he simply asked if he might present two of her own countrymen—Lord Hertford's son, Mr. Edward Conway and his friend, Major-General O'Hara who had just arrived in Rome.

O'Hara!

The sound of that name affected her in a very odd way.

Mr. Conway was making his bow. A delicate-looking man with a sensitive face but one which made hardly an impression on her.

O'Hara's was a face she would never forget even though she saw it through a blur for the very mention of his name brought back that evening at the Cowpers so forcefully that she felt almost faint.

That dimly lighted room, her despairing sob and the sudden emergence of the comforter from the shadows—the stranger passing by!

Now they were face to face under the Cardinal's blazing chandeliers. His bow was courtly, his greeting formal and correct and he gave no sign of recognising her.

"Do you stay long in Rome, General O'Hara?" she enquired presently.

"Until June, I expect. We plan to reach home by the autumn. And you?"

"We are to live for a time in France when we leave Italy. My father wishes us to perfect our knowledge of the language and he also desires my sister to take extra drawing lessons. She has a great natural ability."

She meant, as always, to give the impression that all their plans emanated from her father and few suspected otherwise, least of all Mr. Berry himself.

"An admirable idea," O'Hara said. Then he went on in a much more eager tone: "Have you seen the city by night, Miss Berry? The view from the Cardinal's balcony is unsurpassed and one can never have enough of it. Do let us step outside for a moment." He offered his arm.

Outside the air was warm and caressing, thousands of lights twinkled in the streets and on the hills and the noise of strident Italian voices came up from the crowds promenading below. On either side of the balcony there were banks of flowers massed in tubs and the smell was delicious and slightly intoxicating.

O'Hara said: "I have thought of you a great deal since our last meeting, Miss Berry. I trust I don't offend you by referring to it—if so I shall never mention it again." His voice was quiet and held a tone of consideration which she liked.

"I thought you had not recognised me!" she exclaimed.

"But you knew me. I saw it in your eyes."

"I should not be likely to forget one who had been so understanding. You were there at the very moment when I most wanted a friend. And besides—"

"Besides what?"

She couldn't say what was in her mind—she was too full of confused thoughts to be able to disentangle one intelligent one. The thing that struck her most forcibly about him was his eyes. They were large and dark and well-shaped, but it was the softness of their expression that distinguished them. Agnes had described him as handsome with a bronze complexion, blue-black chin and the most dazzling white teeth she had ever seen. This was all indisputable, but she hadn't mentioned his eyes.

"I didn't expect we should meet again," she said.

"If you would rather we didn't you have only to say so," he replied. "If my presence is unwelcome pray let me know it for the last thing in the world I would wish is to embarrass you."

"I beg you to think no such thing," she cried. "You inspired me with courage when I was at my lowest ebb and I've been grateful to you ever since. I'm glad of the chance to say so and to thank you with all my heart.''

''And I'm delighted to see you looking as radiant and exquisite as Miss Gore assured me you were. I heard a great deal about you, Miss Berry—and all of it good, let me hasten to add.''

''Heavens above, how depressing! I must be a cypher if everyone said the same thing!'' she exclaimed.

''You must let me know you better and be my own judge of that,'' he said. ''I assure you I shan't be influenced by anything I hear—good or bad.''

''I'm honoured by your interest,'' she said, making a little curtsey. ''I've heard something of you, too, and I shan't be influenced either, I promise you.''

''Miss Berry, I think you're laughing at me!''

''General O'Hara, I wouldn't dare!''

''I have a feeling we understand each other quite remarkably. We shall laugh at the same things.''

''And cry at the same things, too?''

''If they're tragic enough to cry over I don't doubt we shall.''

They rejoined the glittering throng and she saw him so much better now and began to feel an ease in his presence that she did not experience with other people. She found it most comfortable.

He was much in demand and was constantly surrounded by men and women who knew him, or had recently met friends of his and they were all anxious for a word or two. By various remarks they made she judged Agnes was right and that he was not far short of their father's age although he carried his years so lightly he could have been taken for a young man.

"How wonderful it would be to have him for an elder brother," she thought to herself. "Or for an uncle. No! Not an uncle. I hate uncles. A brother! What a help it would be to have someone really masculine in the family!"

The chance presently came for her to tell Agnes she found General O'Hara prepossessing.

"They say he's a terrible man for the women," Agnes whispered.

"That's his own affair—and theirs. I like him very much and should like to know him better."

The Cardinal was talking to O'Hara and Mr. Conway when Mr. Berry disengaged himself from the group he was with to collect his daughters and take their leave. It was long after midnight.

"General O'Hara means to explore St. Peter's tomorrow," the Cardinal said. "He's determined to see everything in one day and won't believe it's impossible."

"I don't mean to examine it stone by stone. Conway and I simply want to gain a general impression," O'Hara protested.

"For that perhaps a day will suffice," the Cardinal conceded. "But only if you have a good guide."

"Will you suggest one?"

"Miss Berry," returned the Cardinal, his little dark eyes twinkling under his heavy brow. "If you can persuade Miss Berry to take you under her wing . . . "

"But I am not an expert!" Mary protested.

The Cardinal patted her hand. "You are sympathetic. You can convey a great deal, ma chére fille."

"May we impose on you then—on all of you?" O'Hara asked.

Mr. Berry took it upon himself to accept. They would be charmed, flattered, delighted to be of service.

"Tomorrow then," O'Hara said, and his gaze met Mary's for an instant with a look of warm appreciation.

As they drove home Mr. Berry and Agnes were in raptures.

"How gratifying to be noticed by such men as General O'Hara and Mr. Conway," he said. "They move in the very best society in London, I hear."

Mary said nothing. She sat back in the carriage thinking what bliss it must be to have a real friend, one with whom she could be as compatible as she had been in her childhood days with the beloved governess who had left them to be married. This was the one person in those dark times that Mary had been able to turn to with her woes and joys for her father and grandmother were far too harassed by their pecuniary cares to bother.

Mary was only twelve years old when the governess left and she wept for weeks because the sense of loss was so crippling. No replacement came for Mr. Berry decided Mary knew quite enough to educate herself from then on. She certainly knew more than the governess but there was no substitute for the warm companionship.

Perhaps now if they were thrown together often enough, she might achieve a friendship with O'Hara. It was an exciting thought for masculinity would give the verve and gusto that friendship with women lacked.

When they reached home Agnes fell into bed exhausted without bothering about her hair but Sally, her pretty face pink and her blue eyes sparkling with excitement, was all ready to wait on Mary.

"You'll never guess who I saw this evening, Miss Mary," she burst out, blushing and smoothing down her dress which had an exceptionally crumpled appearance.

"You saw Rory," Mary replied.

"Lawks! However did you guess?"

"That would be telling," Mary said, but Sally looked so bewildered, so happy and so taken aback that Mary couldn't resist hugging her and saying: "There, you goose! Let him be as much in love with you as he dares! We're going to St. Peter's with General O'Hara tomorrow all day so if Rory doesn't contrive to spend some time with you I shall think him a mighty dull fellow."

4

IT WAS AFTERNOON and although the sun was hot on the steps of St. Peter's the air was cold at the top of the dome. Mary had gone tripping up the narrow stairway with O'Hara making heavy weather at her heels as he twisted his great frame round tortuous bends and stooped double to avoid the low roof.

Mr. Berry with Agnes and Mr. Conway had elected to go no further than the terrace over the Basilica but Mary wanted to see the view from the top.

"There!" she exclaimed, when they emerged in the open, "would you have missed this for the world?"

"Not for many worlds. And in this particular one you and I are alone!"

"And we can look down like gods, can't we? See how the air sparkles just as though it's splintered with diamonds and was there ever such a sky? So flawless a blue! When I see beauty like this I could almost grow good!"

She was gazing about her unaware that O'Hara's interest was in observing her and not the panorama.

"Miss Berry, I'm perfectly certain that you are good already, but you puzzle me maddeningly, and have done since the day we met," he said.

"There's no mystery about me at all—unless it amuses you to make one. I have one misfortune. I was not born a boy."

"The misfortune would have fallen on men if you had been!" he cried. "We should have been the poorer."

"But Papa would have been rich. Gorgeously, lavishly, sumptuously, extravagantly rich! Think of that, General O'Hara."

"And your sex debars him from this? I think I've heard something of this from others."

"I'm sure you have for the story preceds us wherever we go and can be twisted and adapted in all manner of ways. Shall I tell you the truth of it?"

"I wish you would," he said.

"It is simply this. My father was idyllically happy until my mother died leaving him with Agnes and me. His uncle, Mr. Ferguson, whose heir he was, desired him to marry again. Mr. Ferguson was set on a male heir to follow my father, you understand. But my poor Papa was so stricken by grief and so faithful to my mother's memory that he would never consider replacing her."

"That is an affecting tribute to her. I respect Mr. Berry the more for it."

"Then you can imagine the feelings Agnes and I cherish for him." She paused a moment and then went on: "But he paid dearly for his fidelity because his younger brother, my uncle William, choused him out, and won old Mr. Ferguson's favour by marrying an heiress and producing sons."

"And he inherited all, I presume?"

"My father was left enough to bring in a mere pittance and his brother, out of sheer shame I think, grants him an annuity that is to die with him. There, General O'Hara, now you know the true story of Robert Berry and his daughters."

"I like it, Miss Berry. I like it immensely—all three of you come out of it with honour. But how can it be twisted to your discredit? Was it not something of the kind that distressed you so much in Florence?"

"Yes, for it was the first time I caught a glimpse of myself as others may see me and it was like looking into a distorting mirror. But it was so mean and false and wicked my feelings boiled over and I spoke up for myself and let the scandalmongers know I'd overheard them."

"Good for you. But having told me so much you must tell me the rest," he said.

So she told him about the musicians' gallery and Mrs. Tristram and what she had said.

"I suppose I've made an enemy for life," she finished.

"Perhaps, but don't let her spoil life for you. Miss Berry, I'm going to risk your anger. Are you a designing woman? Most women are, you know."

She felt a little startled and tried to fathom his expression unsuccessfully. Then she decided to be strictly honest. She wanted him to know her mind exactly.

"I try to do what is wisest and best for my family and I don't think there's anything to be ashamed of in that," she said.

"Nor do I," he agreed in a tone of admiration. "I applaud you." Then he went on: "But forgive me for observing that you talk as though you are the man of the family."

"I am," she told him. "I can admit it up here in this world where we are alone and everything we say is carried away by the wind. But when we rejoin the others you must forget it."

"That's more than I can promise. But I'll never speak of it. Will that content you?"

"Yes, since I'm sure I can trust you."

She could not understand why she felt such confidence in this dark and powerful-looking man. He was looking at her with such an odd expression, too. It was almost as though he was fighting something back—as though he wanted to tell her something in his turn. If he did he evidently overcame the desire for he smiled at her in a fraternal way that she found most comforting.

She felt suddenly quite deliciously happy and said impulsively:

"I like older men, General O'Hara! I find them so much more sympathetic. Perhaps that's why I

can talk to you as to no one else!"

He gave a wry smile. "Thank you," he said. "I needed that to keep me in my senses."

"Are you in danger of losing them?" she teased. "Is it this intoxicating Rome air or is it because we're so high off the ground? Don't lose your senses, I beg, for you're such good company in them I doubt if I'd like you so much if you were minus."

"Have no fear. I've kept them these many years," he said abruptly. "Come, we'd better go down. It's grown icy."

For a moment she feared she had offended him, but when he took her hand to help her down the narrow way there was something in his manner that dispelled her qualms.

And whenever they met, as they did almost every day in the weeks that followed, she knew by his every word and action that he wanted her to know she had not misplaced her confidence in him.

It was a wonderful, exciting, exuberant spring. Mary had never imagined life could be so packed with sheer enjoyment, or that there were so many pleasant and friendly people in the world.

They went sightseeing with other visitors almost every day and O'Hara accompanied them except on the occasions when pain from the wounds he had sustained in the American war kept him to his lodging. The thought of his suffering worried Mary but Rory MacCarthey guarded him like a watchdog, watching over him and keeping everyone else at bay.

"He's most possessive," Mary said, but O'Hara spoke highly of this man and laughed over his numerous amours.

"A red-headed brat appears nine months to the dot in every town we pass through," he said. "The world's peppered with MacCartheys."

Mary thought about this and decided it was her duty to pass the information on to Sally as tactfully as she could, but the maid received it with indignation, grew very red in the face and replied:

"I know as you mean well by warning me only as it happens Rory has told me all that himself. And from what he says the General's no angel either."

"Well, that doesn't concern either you or me, Sally," returned Mary rather stiffly.

"The General hates women—except to go to bed with. He's got no time for 'em at all," Sally went on. "He says they're all the same—every one."

"Thank you, Sally. I prefer to draw my own conclusions," Mary said.

"I know you do, Miss. And I like to draw mine."

Mary couldn't help feeling put out by what Sally had said but as O'Hara's conduct was no concern of hers she tried not to dwell on it. So far as she and Agnes were concerned he couldn't have been more courteous and considerate and he never gave them the least indication of feeling contempt for womankind.

June came far too quickly and their last few days were spent in a hectic round of farewells to the friends they were leaving behind. O'Hara was concerned for his friend, Conway, whose delicate health had prevented him from entering into many of their activities. Mary saw them both at Cardinal de Bernis' where they spent their last evening and noticed how feverish and unwell Mr. Conway looked.

"As we are leaving in the morning and travelling the same road I don't propose to say goodbye to you," O'Hara said.

"Morning's almost here!" exclaimed Mary. "I should be supervising the packing but I left Sally in charge and she's so capable I think I can forget it."

But when she got home she found Sally sitting on the floor in floods of tears with nothing done.

"Why, what on earth's the matter?" she cried.

Sally gulped and snuffled and stuck her fists in her eyes but the tears still ran down.

"I don't want to leave you, Miss Mary," she said, blurting the words out between her sobs.

"You're not going to leave me, you silly goose," Mary said. "Why should you talk of it?"

"Because—oh lawks, Miss, I've gone and got married! I'm a married woman and must go where my husband takes me."

"Married? What in the world are you telling me?" Mray cried. Suddenly her conscience smote her. While she had been carried away by the excitement of every day she had forgotten all about Sally's interest in the amorous Rory MacCarthey.

"Sally, you haven't married General O'Hara's man, have you?" she cried.

"I have. We were married as soon as ever the

General came to Rome, and now I'm three months gone! Oh, Miss Mary, I'm that scared!''

"You're not afraid I'll be cross, are you, Sally?" she asked gently, for the girl looked really frightened.

"I'm scared of having a baby and I'm scared of what the General will do. He'll be so angry with Rory,'' Sally replied shakily.

"You may leave the General to me," said Mary. "I shall see that you're properly taken care of, but why in the world didn't you tell me?"

"I was afraid you'd talk me out of it," Sally said. "I knew you'd give me all sorts of reasons why I should stop and think and I didn't want to hear 'em.''

Mary smiled. "I daresay I might have done,'' she said. "But now I wish you happiness with all my heart. Rory is a very lucky man and I hope he knows it.''

"He keeps telling me he does," and Sally, sitting back on her heels and drying her tears. A seraphic look came over her face.

"The tales he can tell!" she exclaimed. "He can talk you into fairyland when he's a mind to. He's as gay and loving as any wife could wish, but he doesn't know what the General will say and with the baby coming we don't know where we are.''

"I'm sure the General will treat him fairly," said Mary. "But he'll be angered by deception if I know anything of him, so Rory had better confess at once and get it over.''

"Oh Miss. I've got such a funny feeling inside!" Sally said, and promptly fainted.

Mary ran to the door and called for Agnes who came in and turned everything upside down in the flurry of finding restoratives which had been packed for the journey.

Hearing the commotion Mr. Berry came to the door and looked quite aghast when he heard what had happened.

"What is to be done?" he asked, feeling in all his pockets and looking at his watch as though he hoped it would tell him the answer.

"We must send for General O'Hara," replied Mary.

"At this time of night?" queried Mr. Berry.

"Yes, indeed. I must be assured that Sally will be honourably treated without delay."

"Of course," Mr. Berry said, and he trundled off bemusedly to the servants' quarters to send someone for the General while Sally, who had regained consciousness although she still looked dazed, lay gazing at Mary and Agnes with a weak smile on her face.

"This funny fluttering in my inside makes me feel so queer as I can't tell you," she murmured.

"It's your baby moving," said Mary comfortingly. "You'll have him kicking away like a ballet dancer before long and once the strangeness wears off you'll be glad."

Agnes set about tidying the room while Mary went on encouraging Sally, but presently they heard voices in the adjoining room, Mr. Berry's and O'Hara's. Sally went pale with apprehension. Then there came a tap at the door and Rory was on the threshold looking half-bold, half-sheepish.

"See what a pretty pass you've brought our Sally to," Mary said sternly. "Marrying her indeed, without a word to her friends! Aren't you ashamed of yourself?"

"No, Madame," answered Rory, looking Mary in the face, his glinting eyes now wide open and startlingly blue. "It's the best day's work I ever did and my master can kick me downstairs if he chooses."

"Oh no, Rory! Your neck would be broken and the baby'll be an orphan before it draws breath!" squealed Sally.

"It's been near enough broken before, but I'll be looking after the both of you till we're all old together," Rory said, dropping on his knees and taking Sally's head on his shoulder.

"We won't ever be parted, will we?" she pleaded.

"I'd like to see who'd try to part us, so I would. He'd have my pity," Rory declared.

Mary signalled Agnes to follow her and they went into the next room where her father and O'Hara were sharing a bottle of wine. She had never seen the General look so put out.

"Well, here's a pretty mess!" he exclaimed angrily, before she could speak. "I never had a woman in my train yet and I don't want one now—especially a pregnant one."

She was completely unprepared for such harshness and bridled at his tone.

"Then what do you propose?" she asked coldly. "Your man has married our Sally and the result is a baby. What else would you expect, General O'Hara?"

She looked at him with such disdain that his eyes flickered away from her.

"Miss Berry, this is not a subject I care to discuss with a lady," he said sulkily.

"Then you must learn to care, for Rory has made Sally his wife and now he must fend for her."

"My man's a dog and deserves whipping like one," O'Hara growled.

"My maid is not to have a whipped husband while I can prevent it," Mary returned.

"Love! Women! I've no time for either. Women are the devil. They're all the same! Sly, crafty, cunning—lying in wait with their wiles and pretty ways that made anyone but the dupe who's under their spell quite sick!"

He was so angry, striding up and down the room, glass in hand, that he slopped wine over his fine coat and didn't even notice.

"Thank you, General O'Hara, and what experience do you speak from?" asked Mary hotly. "Not one you'd be proud to own, I fancy. I've heard you have a low opinion of women and I would not believe it. Now I see I was wrong."

"Miss Berry!" There was a note of alarm in O'Hara's voice.

"I can have no more to say to you—nor can Agnes either," Mary said. "We will leave you to confer with my father, but if you fail to settle matters to my satisfaction you will have to bargain for more than you reckon for."

"Good heavens, child, don't go!" cried Mr. Berry, alarmed at the prospect of a decision being left to him. "What are you all in such a pet about?"

"You must ask the General, Papa," replied

Mary looking O'Hara coolly up and down.

"Miss Berry, Miss Agnes, I implore you not to take to yourselves what I let fly in the heat of the moment!" exclaimed O'Hara. "It did not apply to you—I never meant it to."

"You should think before you explode, General O'Hara. Especially on such a subject," Mary said.

He kept looking at her so miserably as he finished his wine that she began to feel sorry for him.

"Let's forget our differences and decide what to do about Sally," she said impetuously.

"My plan of setting off with Conway is already fixed. We haven't engaged a carriage."

"But as we travel the same way she shall have her usual seat in ours," Mary said. "Rory may ride with you and you won't be in the least upset. At Chamonix we can make further arrangements— and those you may leave to me."

"Miss Berry, I beg you not to think of my comfort—you made me ashamed," he said. "But you must surely see the trouble the silly wench has caused by diving into a bachelor's establishment?"

"That's a risk all single men must take—master and man alike," Mary replied. "But I think you may depend upon us all being quite contented."

She spoke lightly and began to go into details of their route which she declared would be delightful and he was soon as enthusiastic about it as she.

"We must spend a day or two in Florence to see Miss Gore—we promised her," she said.

"And your bête noire, Mr. Tristram?" he asked.

"I shall avoid her."

"She has a nephew from London with her, I

fear. You'll fall in love with him, for sure!''

''No doubt of it if he's the one you told me of!''

''He is—with slate-grey eyes, no eyelashes, and lips the same colour as his face, only wet.''

''Urgh!''

''He spends all his time trying to ingratiate himself with people who don't want to know him and revenges himself on them by supplying snippets of scandal to the newspapers.''

''I shall never be able to resist him! Oh, I was forgetting—we must go to Terni to see the waterfall on the way. Don't you agree? But after that it will soon be Chamonix where we must part.''

They had both forgotten their flare-up. Mr. Berry had fallen asleep in his chair and Agnes was busy in the next room going through her sketches and packing those she wanted to keep.

''Mary—don't let us part at Chamonix. Come with us all the way. I shall be cursed dull without you.''

She was touched by the way he spoke and to hear him call her Mary. Her name seemed to come so naturally from him it was as though he had never really thought of her as Miss Berry at all. She managed not to show her surprise.

''But we must go to Montpellier,'' she explained. ''Living there will be so cheap—and we can get some education as well. Agnes and I have been dreadfully neglected and we shall have to work really hard to improve. I feel my ignorance dreadfully at times. There now! Who could I say a thing like that to but you?''

''You honour me. But you dash my hopes at the

same time, Mary. Will it be long before we meet again?''

"I suppose it must be."

She sighed because the prospect of going all the way with him was enticing, but it was useless to think of what they could not afford.

"You won't be harsh with poor Sally, will you?" she said.

"No, I promise you."

He took a turn about the room, came to a halt by her chair and said abruptly: "When we meet again I suppose you, too, will be married! You will be a countess at least!"

She laughed. "What optimism!" she said. "I've no romantic illusions and what use would they be if I had? Earls marry to increase their estates, not to diminish them. Besides, whoever takes me must take Pa and Agnes as well."

"But you'll make a good, prudent marriage before long."

"Prudence will be my last consideration," she said. "I think the best thing I can do is to make myself an agreeable woman of the world."

He roared laughing.

"Oh, I mean it," she said. "I've thought a great deal about it since I heard that poisonous old Mrs. Tristram talking. No one shall ever accuse me of husband hunting, but if I learn as much as I can and become companionable and pleasant enough to be wanted on my own merits I shan't complain. And when I'm old I may even have a salon where all the wits and beaux will congregate."

"And where dukes and statesmen and men and

women of learning will compete for invitations, eh?''

She saw a picture of just such a salon. ''Will you be there?'' she asked. ''The door will always be open to you.''

He looked as though she were worlds away.

''When you are old, Mary, I shall be dead.''

His words sent a chill through her. ''Oh no! Life would be cold without you!'' she cried.

''What do you wish for most in the world? Riches, power, love?'' he asked.

The hills were silhouetted against the sky as dawn broke and the lights were going out in all the great houses where parties and receptions had been going on all night.

She looked into his face and saw devotion and steadfastness there. She could speak with complete sincerity.

''I wish for a friend more than for anything else in the world,'' she said. ''One who will accept me as I am, forgive me my prickliness and my conceits, understand why I am thin-skinned and easily hurt—one I can turn to with all my troubles and doubts and miseries. That is what I wish for most.''

He took a long time to think of this but at last he said: ''You have that friend in me, Mary.''

He took her hand.

''You make me very happy, O'Hara.''

His words, the touch of his hand, his sincerity, filled her with gratitude and affection and she wanted him to know it.

''It will be reciprocal, won't it?'' she asked.

"Let me be as much your friend as you promise to be mine. Or would that displease you?"

"It pleases me," he said. "And it satisfies me as well—for the present."

He lifted her hand, which he still held, to his lips, looked deep into her eyes and, with a smile that left her wondering, he went away.

5

MARY AND AGNES spent hours discussing where their Zoffany portrait should be hung when they at last returned to London and took a house in Somerset Street. Mr. Berry had no doubts on the subject at all. It was to have the place of honour over the drawing-room fireplace and he wouldn't hear any argument against it.

So everyone who called was naturally drawn to look at it and one day when Mary came home from a shopping expedition she found O'Hara there, so engrossed in studying it that he didn't hear her come in.

She stood in the doorway, her heart beating rather faster than usual. It was so long since they had parted—two years, or was it three?

"O'Hara!"

He wheeled round looking as though he had been startled out of a dream, recollected himself, made her a sweeping bow and said:

"Why, my dear Mary!" And then, after a long look: "Upon my word I scarcely knew you for a moment! You're so fashionable and so elegant and so grown-up!"

"You didn't expect me to look like that picture still, did you?" she asked. "I was a chubby sixteen when Zoffany painted it."

"It's charming—just as you were when we first met. How glad I am to see you again! And now I look harder I see that you're still the same—except for a few external trimmings. A jolly little girl with a most engaging smile."

"I was a very cross little girl when that was done," she told him. "I was seething with anger because Pa had been cheated and if Zoffany hadn't made me laugh with his tales of Italy which he related in the vilest accent you ever heard, you'd see a perfectly horrid little face up there—sour as a crab apple."

"I shall never believe it. But you haven't said you're pleased to see me!"

"How can you doubt it? Do let us sit down and be comfortable," she said. "I haven't forgotten one moment of our happy days in Rome, or of your kindness to us when we all left it together. Do you remember the waterfall at Terni and how we stood under it and felt as though we were surrounded by rainbows?"

"You made me walk six miles to see it," he said.

"You never complained."

"How could I? You were so deliciously enthralled by it all."

"And so were you. Admit it."

"I do, with complete candour. I only wish occasions like that came oftener. Since those days you've been physically elusive, Mary. Your letters have told me much—but not everything, I'll be bound."

"I might say the same of yours."

"Ah! You can't make out my atrocious hand. Come, confess it."

"Oh yes I can—and do. But I'd rather hear your voice any day."

"And so you might have done if you had not spent so much time gallivanting all over Europe, and then the moment you came home you were off to Yorkshire . . ."

"To see my grandmother . . ."

"And to Scotland . . ."

"Where our wicked Uncle William enjoys the estates that ought to have been Pa's. We didn't see Uncle William, by the way. I don't think we could have borne to behold the magnificence he choused us out of, and anyway, he didn't invite us. Just fancy! There was a time when I was so green I thought he would!"

She was laughing at the idea but he didn't join in. His look was compassionate and he said gently:

"My dear Mary, I think you still feel these pricks as sharp as ever. I know how they can hurt." He paused a moment and then went on: "But I hear on all sides that the Berrys are in great demand in society and have been ever since they came back from the continent. Oh, I hear a great deal of you!"

"So it seems. But what of you? I want news, too, and it's hard to come by. Do you remember you once asked me what I wished for most?"

"Indeed I do—and your answer."

"I've often been comforted since in knowing I have your friendship. When things go wrong, I think 'O'Hara would understand,' and at once I feel better. But I reproach myself, too, for I never asked if you had a wish."

He paused before he replied, looking at her gravely, and then he said:

"Mary, as a young man I served under Lord Tyrawley in Gibraltar. I was Quartermaster-General of troops. I can't describe the feelings that sometimes came over me, but I determined one day to become Governor of the Rock. My birth, my lack of fortune spur me on to succeed, to overcome my drawbacks and yet I feel I've achieved little—and in so long a time."

"Don't take time into account," she said warmly. "You will attain your ambition for sure."

"To no one but you could I speak of these things. With you alone I can sink my pride," he said, in a tone that affected her deeply.

"If you knew how deeply your confidence touches me . . . " she began.

"We have both felt the slings and arrows," he said with a laugh. "And now we meet again it's as though we never parted."

"We're as comfortable together as ever we were

and you must promise to come often," she said.

"Ah, that's the pity of it. I'm in transit—or shall be soon. I am posted to Gibraltar."

"Then preferment must come soon!" she exclaimed. "Oh, I hope it will. I shall set my mind on it for you."

Voices in the hall interrupted their confidences as Agnes came in followed by her father and they both welcomed O'Hara warmly for although his friendship with Mary was particular he was counted a member of the family by all three and soon they were talking all at once as they indulged in the pleasures of reunion.

Mary listened rather more than she spoke. There was laughter at such topics as the size of Sally's family for she had been merely pregnant when they parted and was now the mother of two children with a third on the way. There was a touch of sadness when they recollected Edward Conway who had died so soon after he and O'Hara reached home.

"I was at least able to restore him to his family and I was thankful for that for I owe the Conways so much more than I can ever repay them," O'Hara said. "I've recently been staying at Henley with my kindest benefactor of that name. Marshal Conway has a seat near the river and is at present building a bridge across it."

"Remarkable! I should much like to see it," Mr. Berry said.

"Ah, but wait. Marshal Conway has a daughter who is a sculptress. Mrs. Damer has carved two heads to ornament the bridge."

"Incredible! A female sculptress?" Mr. Berry was astounded.

"My dear sir, have a care! She's passable at making plaster dogs but Mr. Walpole will have it that she's a second Bernini! He's partial to her as she's his kinswoman so his rhapsodies must be taken with a pinch of salt as I daresay you've learned."

"We don't happen to know Mr. Walpole," Mary said.

"Good heavens! You must be the only people in London who don't!" exclaimed O'Hara.

"I gather that he does not wish to meet *us*," returned Mary crisply.

"That's remarkable!"

"Is it?"

She was on the verge of indignation as she spoke, but realising she would spoil the pleasant atmosphere if she gave way to it she said quickly:

"Do tell us more about Mrs. Damer. I never met a sculptress."

"Nor I," chimed in Mr. Berry. "She must be very agile."

O'Hara roared laughing. "She's almost as full of wounds as I am. She falls off her ladder every other day."

"How unkind to laugh," Mary said. "I think it's wonderful to create. I only wish I could."

"I daresay you could," O'Hara remarked.

O'Hara's reappearance added excitement to their enterprises for he accompanied them everywhere and hardly a day went by but they met for a drive, or at the theatre, or some reception.

One autumn day when the sun was shining Agnes suggested driving to Hammersmith to see if Sally had her new gown ready.

"If she has I shall wear it at Lady Herries tonight," she said.

Sally was established in a cottage she had bought with a legacy from her grandfather. It was within a stone's throw of Chiswick Mall which Mary remembered as the scene of their drabbest years when they waited and hoped for the fortune that never came.

For her it was associated with bills and deprivations and an atmosphere of gloom and her chief solace had been the innumerable books that littered the old house. But Sally's presence in the neighbourhood had dispelled the sadder recollections and Mary always enjoyed going to see her, for despite her growing family Sally had become a devotee of fashion and loved to hear news of the brilliant world she only saw from the outside.

O'Hara needed no persuasion to accompany them on the drive and soon they were clattering along bowing to the friends they passed on the way. Their carriage was extremely elegant and was drawn by the glossiest horses which they could never have afforded without Mary's economies. She was elated in possessing it and as they left Kensington behind and took the road through the laden orchards she breathed a sigh of contentment. It was all so beautiful! The trees bearing down with fruit, the women with great baskets of it on their heads trudging the road to market. So much colour and such a delicious scent in the air. "A scene for Agnes to paint," she said.

A rider entering London drew rein as they passed, hesitated behind them and then galloped back.

"Oh God! A highwayman!" Agnes exclaimed.

But the rider was up beside them. "O'Hara! By all that's miraculous, it is O'Hara!" he cried. "I thought I couldn't mistake that laugh!"

O'Hara, nonplussed for an instant, recognised the newcomer as he finished speaking.

"Why Barnes! I took you for a robber, upon my soul I did!" he exclaimed. "Good God, man, to think we should meet at last—and in London! This is a far cry from York Town."

And with this he begged leave to introduce Mr. Barnes, a fellow officer who had been with him in the American war when the English had been forced by famine to surrender to General Washington.

Mary knew that as Lord Cornwallis had been too ill to relinquish his sword to the conqueror in person on that occasion it had fallen to O'Hara to represent him and she always felt sad to think of so valiant a soldier riding out at the head of the vanquished army with the band playing "The World's Turned Upside Down Again."

But the inevitable recollections meeting with Mr. Barnes brought him did not dash O'Hara's spirits and he told his friend he had been on a mission to Jamaica since then. "But the minute I set foot in England again my creditors were after me like a pack of wolves so I beat a retreat to Italy where I had the great felicity of meeting the Miss Berrys," he said.

Upon this, knowing that the two men must have much to say to each other, Mary asked Mr. Barnes to turn and ride with them to Sally's.

"Pray don't mind Agnes and me," she said, "but forgive us if we listen. O'Hara tells us so little of his exploits we depend on his friends to learn if he ever went to war."

Mr. Barnes laughed. "He had a roll of drums for a lullaby and a war-horse for a nurse and he carries more scars than you ever had nettle stings. He was on a battlefield when you two were mere toddlers and he's the best and finest man I ever served under."

"If you're going to persist in talking of me pray lend me your horse, my dear fellow, and take my place in the carriage," O'Hara said, and Mary almost wished Mr. Barnes would accept the offer and satisfy her curiosity, but he took the hint and changed the subject.

Sally was hanging out lines of washing when her visitors arrived and she came to the door in her coarse apron all wet with suds. Freddie, her first born and Molly her second peeped out from behind her, their eyes round with wonder.

"Why, Miss Mary! Just look at me! And there's the General, too. I'm that ashamed to be caught like this, Miss Agnes, dear! Freddie, make your bow to the Miss Berrys like I taught you."

The little boy executed an extraordinary contortion and Mary had to hold her breath to stop from laughing. O'Hara's face was so set that she guessed he wanted to laugh, too, but he said with the utmost gravity:

"You're doing very well, young fellow, but if you put your left hand so, and make a movement like this with your right—then draw your foot back, so, you'll do even better. Capital! You're an excellent pupil, my boy."

The child did his best to imitate the courtly bow O'Hara demonstrated and Mary's amusement was checked. She had never seen him with children before and his courtesy to Sally's son touched her. The warm flood of gratitude because she could count him her friend intensified and she had to turn away as unexpected tears pricked her eyelids. "How odd to be so emotional," she thought.

Sally had the gown almost ready for Agnes and while it was being tried on the others went into the garden and sat under the apple tree and talked and although O'Hara clamped down whenever Mr. Barnes recollected instances of his valour Mary succeeded in learning of quite a few before they reached home again.

6

MARY STILL FELT the exhilaration of the afternoon at Lady Herries that evening. She knew she looked well and so did Agnes and it was obvious they were provoking even more comment than usual.

Agnes was on her father's arm, she was escorted by O'Hara and the first acquaintance to greet them was Mrs. Tristram's nephew, Thomas Gilbert, who they now met almost everywhere they went.

"Don't forget he'll be on the look-out for scandal for the newspapers," O'Hara said in an undertone.

"My dear, charming Miss Berrys!" Mr. Gilbert cried, darting forward the moment they entered and making an extravagant bow, "What new conquests are we to see tonight, I wonder? How many ships will you launch with your bright eyes?''

"As we have four eyes between us I should say we might manage two thousand,'' Mary said coolly. ''But we've nowhere to send 'em, Mr. Gilbert, so I think they may as well stay in port.''

Mr. Gilbert cackled loudly and turned to a young lady who was eyeing the Berrys with a mixture of curiosity and envy.

"What do you think of them?'' he whispered.

"Pushing,'' she said.

"Bide your time, my dear. We'll see how self-possessed they are presently for I believe they're going to take a tumble, and to tell the truth, I can't wait to see it.''

"Oh?'' she said. ''Do let me into the secret!''

"Mr. Walpole's expected and he won't meet them,'' he replied. ''It's the truth, upon my word. He's refused before, you know.''

"No!'' she exclaimed. ''Do you really mean it?''

"It's all round the town,'' he said.

"But on what ground?''

"Why, he says he's heard so much praise of them they must be full of affectation and insipidity. He won't go near them. And the joke of it is they're taking a house at Twickenham!''

"My God! If he won't know them there all his neighbours will avoid them, too!'' she exclaimed.

"They'll be quite ostracised, and won't that be entertaining?'' he tittered. ''Oh, do look. Here's Mr. Walpole coming in the door. Now we shall see something!''

"I believe Mr. Gilbert's talking about us," Mary said in an undertone.

"Then it's just as well we can't hear what he says," replied O'Hara. "Good heavens! That's Mr. Walpole's voice! I'd no idea he was coming."

As the guests seated themselves to listen to a recital on the harpsichord Lady Herries bustled forward to greet the latest arrival who was heard to apologise because the crush of traffic at Hyde Park had held him up for an hour.

"A herd of goats, my dear Lady Herries," he said. "Poor, pretty creatures! It quite dashed my spirits to hear their piteous voices!"

"Dear Mr. Walpole, you care too much for dumb animals," Lady Herries protested.

"Not so dumb. I sometimes think them more eloquent than we are," he said.

"Sit by me," Mary begged O'Hara. "Don't leave my side. I shall die if I'm snubbed."

She looked back to where her father and Agnes sat, wishing they were all four in a row, but she felt safe with O'Hara beside her and as her next neighbour engaged her in conversation, demanding her full attention, she was not aware that Lady Herries had brought Mr. Walpole over, putting O'Hara in a dilemma. There was nothing for him to do but rise and help the old man into the seat their hostess clearly expected him to vacate.

The music began and Mary turned her head and was motionless as she listened. O'Hara leaned against the wall and watched her. Her face, in repose, was exquisite, yet when she spoke and laughed and the soft colour came into her cheeks he would see an even more exciting beauty. Any day some man of wealth and position would realise what a prize she was and offer her hand. He had a dread that he was bound to lose her.

She had still not moved, but now he noticed Mr. Walpole was not watching the performer. His bright eyes were on Mary and there was a look of admiration in them such as O'Hara had never seen him bestow on anyone. It was as though a pair of young eyes was looking out of that old face and the picture was so arresting it conjured up a vision in O'Hara's mind and he saw Walpole as he must have been in youth—and in love. He saw a gay and witty young man with an air that compensated for his lack of looks and lent his irregular features distinction. It was a lively, fascinating face.

And what tones were in his voice when he spoke to the girl he had once loved. What gentleness and ardour might there not have been—and what self-less devotion. He was capable of deep, unswerv-ing affection and his lifelong friendship for his cousin, Marshal Conway, proved it—so how much greater would his love for a woman be—for he had undoubtedly loved and lost in a summer long ago.

But now he was gazing at Mary Berry with those brilliant, youthful eyes of his and he had forgotten his gouty hands and his creaking old body and all the gimcrack baubles at Strawberry Hill and he was in his twenties again, fresh from Cambridge with the world to win and a great name to per-petuate.

O'Hara shifted his weight from one foot to the

other and mopped his brow. He could have sworn he'd been dozing. He'd had a crazy dream about Walpole in which it seemed the old man had recaptured his youth and fallen in love, not with an unknown of long ago, but with Mary Berry.

The recital ended. There was a burst of applause and Mary turned rapturously to O'Hara and found Mr. Walpole in his place. Her lips were opened to speak, but she drew back and her colour deepened. There was an endless moment. Then O'Hara saw her smile and her expression touched his heart with its tenderness. He guessed Walpole wouldn't be able to resisit.

He had only to take two steps to join them and he was relieved to find they were talking quite easily about the music. Mary said she hadn't a notion of what it was all about but the dexterity of the performer's hands fascinated her.

Mr. Walpole presumed that she played an instrument herself.

"Heavens no!" declared Mary. "I never was taught."

"Few young ladies would own that," Walpole remarked.

Mary's eyes twinkled. "When most girls were acquiring such talents I was melting down candle ends and setting them in moulds with string through their middles for wicks. They never answered very well—they weren't in the least like wax candles, but Papa said they were well enough to read by."

O'Hara stood by Mary's chair, his hand on the back of it. He waited his chance to join in.

"So your father likes to read," observed Mr. Walpole, drawing her out.

"Indeed he does, and so do Agnes and I," replied Mary. "We spent our childhood knee-deep in books. We would be up in the loft or down in the cellar or even in an apple tree reading them as hard as we could go."

"Did you choose prose or poetry?"

"Both—and we adore plays. Especially Congreve's. I shall write a play myself one day! We knew 'The Way of the World' by heart and always squabbled over who should be Millamant. I usually won. I'm a year older, of course. But Mirabell's a good part. I didn't mind being Mirabell and strutting about and posing and feeling superior as I fancied myself a man."

"One of these days we'll stage another reading and I shall be Mirabell," O'Hara put in. "You and I would make excellent foils for each other, Mary."

"Why not Beatrice and Benedick?" suggested Mr. Walpole. "A soldier's part would suit you to perfection, O'Hara."

There was no chance to explore the idea as Lady Herries came over and said: "I'm so glad to see you already know my dear Miss Berry, Mr. Walpole. She's so much in demand I almost didn't get her."

A soft look came over Walpole's face as his hostess left them and he said in a gentle tone:

"Miss Berry, I might have had this pleasure before, but I was afraid of it. I'd heard such tales of you and your sister I thought you must be all pretension. You've been cried up to the skies!"

"By whom?" asked Mary in great surprise.

"By O'Hara for the most part. He speaks of your fluent French, your excellent Italian, and your knowledge of Latin, too. Is that not enough to frighten an old man who's forgotten all he ever knew?"

Mary glanced at O'Hara who scowled darkly, looked away and appeared to pretend he had not heard.

"Oh, he makes everyone die to meet you! But I refused to be drawn. I've let it be known I'm far too settled to be disturbed."

"And now?" she asked.

"I succumb."

Lady Herries' guests had noticed the attention Walpole was bestowing on Mary and she thought it was time to give place to others. She excused herself to join her father and Agnes, but as she rose from her seat Mr. Walpole beckoned O'Hara and she heard a sibilant whisper:

"I'd never have believed it. She's completely unaffected!"

"Irresistible," O'Hara said.

"An angel," declared Walpole.

Mary smiled blissfully. How absurd they were and yet how delightful! An angel, irresistible! How Pa and Agnes would laugh.

O'Hara had followed her and she said: "You deserted me."

"I couldn't help it, I swear. Ask Lady Herries."

"There's no need. You're forgiven."

The evening was not yet over. Mary had scarcely rejoined her family when Lady Herries came to say that Mr. Walpole desired to meet Mr. Berry and his younger daughter.

She soon became aware that there were others in the room who felt slighted. In that elegant assembly, they, above all others, had been singled out for special attention and it was impossible not to respond to an old man who was showing a kindliness and good humour she had not expected him to extend to them.

"You once told me he was waspish," she whispered to O'Hara.

"I only said he could be," O'Hara replied.

"I shall believe that when he stings me."

"Then beware. Wasp stings have been known to kill." His voice was hard and his expression melancholy.

"What's the matter? Are you tired of the evening?" she asked.

"I never tire when you are near me," he said, "but I have a premonition. I feel as though a shadow has fallen on us."

"Is that your Gaelic second sight?" she laughed, and then she wished she hadn't for he gave a shudder and she knew he was distressed by something.

He had seen the look on Walpole's face, but he could not speak of it to her, so he tried his best to throw off his mood and managed to persuade her he had done so after a while.

Before the evening ended Mr. Walpole invited the Berrys to Strawberry Hill. "You must come on a summer's day and I shall take pleasure in showing you round myself," he said.

"This is indeed an honour, sir," said Mr. Berry, scarcely able to believe their luck. "We shall look forward to it."

"But we shall meet before then I hope, Mr. Berry. At my age another summer may never come. You must all come to me at Berkeley Square."

Mary thought the room sounded like a beehive for everyone was buzzing with the news of their special invitation to Strawberry and precious few people were given that distinction these days.

"He's absolutely charming," she said to O'Hara. "I hope you'll be with us when we go to Strawberry Hill."

"You forget. I shall be in Gibraltar," he said. "Ah, he's beckoning me."

She was surrounded by a bevy of eager questioners as O'Hara joined Mr. Walpole who chuckled and said: "I exonerate you. Your two Berrys are as delightful as you said and I don't know which is the prettier. Perhaps the elder. Yes, her face is perfect. Can't you see her as the heroine of a romantic novel?"

"There's not a scrap of romance in her—or so she tells me," replied O'Hara.

"An unromantic young lady? Remarkable. Still, it saves us the trouble of looking for a hero, doesn't it? You know, I don't think we'd find one. I don't see anyone here to match her, do you? I'll tell you what! We'll put her in a comedy. What do you say to that?"

"If you intend her for comedy make sure she hasn't got a heart," O'Hara said.

"You're quoting me!"

"With reason. I think she has much feeling. So life could prove a tragedy for her."

"No, no. Comedy's the thing. Genteel comedy. O'Hara, I can scarcely wait to know the charming Berrys better."

"I suppose you've cut another colt's tooth?"

Walpole laughed. "I decided years ago that when I reached eighty I'd try to behave as though I was forty and I'm only seventy, O'Hara. So if you've a head for sums—which I haven't—you may find I'm younger than you are!"

O'Hara saw the old man into his carriage and returned to his part feeling thoroughly out of sorts, especially as Agnes talked of no one but Mr. Walpole all the way home and didn't know how to wait for the proposed visit to Strawberry.

"Next summer's a long way off—you don't suppose he'll forget it, do you?" she asked.

"I'll wager my last guinea he won't. He's fallen in love with you both," O'Hara said.

Mary said that was an absurd notion. "But I don't know why you should sound so cross about it," she added.

She couldn't see his face but she knew he felt put out and tried to mollify him.

"People are always falling in love with us both," she sighed. "That's the trouble, isn't it, Agnes? They even fall in love with us as an entire family."

"So considerate of them," murmured Mr. Berry sleepily.

"Yes," said O'Hara. "Yes, I know."

Mary sensed a note of foreboding in his voice,

but it was so slight she could not question it or guess that he was apprehensive because he saw how strongly Walpole was attracted to her and knew that if he chose to exert his charm and draw her into his enchanted world she might become enslaved and when she woke to her danger it would be too late.

7

MARY VERY SOON found that Mr. Walpole's attraction to them was no passing fancy. There followed a winter that she never forgot for she and Agnes were singled out for his particular attention and they were both so intrigued by his conversation on the first evening they spent with him at his house in Berkeley Square and he was so enraptured to see their pleasure that he invited them again, and then again, and before they knew what had happened they were indispensable to him.

He distilled his reminiscences for their delight and Mary was dazzled by his brilliant word-pictures and entranced by the scenes he conjured up for her.

Those delightful maids of honour who attended

on the Princess of Wales and were clever and fascinating enough to attract the most brilliant men of their day became almost tangible as he described them. She fanced she could hear the rustle of a gown, distant laughter, almost—but almost—catch snatches of their conversation.

And the King's German mistresses! How she and Agnes laughed over them. "Do tell us more!" she begged.

And he did.

He also went about telling everyone he met there was no satisfaction in the world to equal an evening spent with the lovely Berrys.

One night when they were at Berkeley Square with O'Hara they met Mrs. Damer who Mr. Walpole introduced as the daughter of his dear cousin, Marshal Conway.

Mary thought that Mrs. Damer must have been lovely as a girl. In middle age she was still handsome but her dark brown hair was streaked with grey and her pale face lined, but her grey-green eyes were bright and she had an up-turned mouth. Her face was a perfect oval, her nose rather long. She had a slight limp and walked with a stick.

"Mrs. Damer has wanted to make your acquaintance ever since she heard how many evenings you've devoted to an old man who talks too much," Mr. Walpole said.

"And I've wanted to meet Mrs. Damer since I heard of the adornments she carved for Henley Bridge," Mary replied.

"They are superb! She is a female Bernini!" Mr. Walpole enthused, but as he moved off O'Hara said mockingly: "What, my dear Lady Stick! Are you yet chiselling?"

Mary noticed a certain stiffening when his eyes and Mrs. Damer's met. There was a tension as between two cats meeting and arching their backs.

"I am, and shall be," Mrs. Damer replied, and she smiled at Mary in a conspiratorial way and said: "O'Hara doesn't like women who do things. He has the most peculiar ideas about us altogether and I can never persuade him that we're rational beings. Perhaps you can."

"If you are going to join forces against me I shall have nothing more to say to either of you," O'Hara said, his face growing rather red.

"But you can't object to the creation of beautiful things, no matter who makes them, can you?" Mary said gently.

"Now isn't that reasonable?" Mrs. Damer asked.

"It may be. But I stick to my opinion that you'd do better if you followed your mother's example and took up embroidery."

"God, O'Hara! Was I born for nothing more ambitious than embroidery?"

"It would save you all this scrambling up and down and falling off ladders and half killing yourself," he said in a more amiable tone.

"But I should waste my training and all the time I have spent learning sculpture and anatomy!" objected Mrs. Damers.

"Anatomy!" spluttered O'Hara. "A woman learning anatomy! I blush for you, Stick!"

And he was blushing, whether from embarrassment or anger Mary couldn't tell, but she was sorry he was antagonistic to Mrs. Damer for before the evening ended she had a satisfying tête-à-tête with her and found they both enjoyed literature and travel and objected to having so few opportunities in life by reason of their sex.

Mrs. Damer gave her a very cordial invitation to visit her studio and see her work which Mary accepted eagerly but on the way downstairs with O'Hara she noticed how he muttered and swore under his breath and asked him why.

"The Stick always rubs me up the wrong way," he said moodily. "I bristle whenever we meet. Yet her parents, Marshal Conway and his wife Lady Ailesbury, are my dearest friends. Mrs. Damer has her merits, I suppose, but I can't get on with her at all."

"I thought her most interesting. She's learning Greek," Mary said.

He stopped short. "She would!" he said. "Well, don't have too much to do with her."

"Why? Are you jealous of her intellect?"

"She's a bad influence," he said.

"Of that I shall judge for myself," replied Mary firmly, for she would not allow anyone to sway her when it came to choosing her friends. However, as he was leaving for Gibraltar so soon she did not want to ruffle him or allow him to go away thinking that anyone else, man or woman, was likely to oust him as her favourite and most appreciated friend. She was going to miss him quite badly.

Down at Hammersmith Sally was not looking forward either to her parting from Rory who had settled down to civilian life and grown quite fat. But his allegiance to his General was unshakable.

"He saved me from the gallows," he often told Sally. "But for him I'd have been turned off before my fifteenth birthday."

Sally always held her throat when he told her this and her eyes popped wide open. Her Rory, her loved and loving Rory, had stolen a loaf when he was starving.

"Go with the General," she told him. "I'll bide by whatever you say, Rory."

"And if it wasn't that the baby's so poorly I'd go too," she told Mary one day when she was turning up the hem of the new gown that was to be worn for the forthcoming visit to Strawberry Hill where Mr. Walpole had promised to show them all his treasures.

The whole family looked forward to this expedition and Agnes talked of nothing else.

"I shall be able to picture you both sitting at his feet when I'm on the high seas," O'Hara remarked one day. "You're like two spellbound children peeping into an unknown world and you're both intoxicated by the wit and gallantry of the people he talks about."

"Don't grudge us the pleasure," Mary said. "Just think how we shall miss you. We must have our compensations!"

"Let me sketch you for remembrance," Agnes said. "Stay there and I'll fetch my things."

She went to her table at the other end of the room and O'Hara said urgently: "Will you truly miss me, Mary?"

"How can you doubt it?" she asked. "But you must allow me new friends. And I think, in honesty, I must tell you that I like Mrs. Damer very much."

He scowled.

"Why don't you approve of her?" Mary asked.

"I don't like disturbing elements. Why, at the Westminster elections she went careering round with the Devonshire House set, pandering for votes. It was most unseemly. I can't think what Marshal Conway was about to allow it! If she'd been my daughter I'd have locked her up."

"You're so old fashioned!" Mary lamented. "You forget a mature woman has a mind of her own—and Mrs. Damer has means of her own, too—lucky creature! And she has such talents. I wish I were half as accomplished as she!"

"Thank God you are as you are," he said gruffly. "You are quite accomplished enough and I only hope you give her a wide berth. She won't do you any good."

"Dear O'Hara, don't let us quarrel," she said. "I shall hate it when you're gone. I shan't have anyone to complain to."

Agnes was absorbed in her task and she was as unaware of what they were saying as he was of her presence.

"You never complain," he said.

"Oh, but I do! I'm always wishing myself powerful and influential instead of a mere Miss ordering household affairs and seeing Pa and Agnes are comfortable and contented and living within our means."

"You do it so discreetly no one ever guesses, and as to power—My God—you have a bigger allowance of that than you know what to do with."

"But real power only comes through men," she objected.

"Then marry one!" he burst out in exasperation.

"Any one? Don't you know me better than that?"

"I think you are too high-flown. You miss chances that are right under your nose."

"Now you're teasing! But confidentially I'll tell you something. When I find the right man—or when he finds me—there'll be such a conflagration as you'll see from Gibraltar. He and I will set the world on fire, O'Hara!"

She expected him to laugh and wondered why his face froze—but it was only for a moment. "What? Is he to put my nose out of joint then?" he asked. "Shall I have no more confidences—no hero's parts to play when you take the heroine's? Do I become the faithful retainer standing humbly to one side and being sent off on a mission only to return at the fall of the curtain in time to dance at your wedding?"

They had played much at amateur theatricals that winter and when Mary teased him by keeping up Millamantish ways after the reading was over he would remind her that he was no Mirabell.

"I'll have none of your cruelty," he said.

"But I'm never cruel to *you*," she objected.

"No?"

"How am I cruel then?"

85

"You give me ideas of heaven."

"That's to the good."

"Is it? Even when it's out of my reach?"

She wondered exactly what he meant. Did he know himself? she asked.

"I believe so," he said, but Agnes brought her sketch book over and said: "I can't get you, O'Hara. You're not an easy subject."

"You've caught Mary's likeness, though. May I have it?" he asked.

She tore the page out and went to put her things away.

"When you are Governor of Gilbraltar Agnes shall do you in oils," Mary whispered.

"I sometimes despair of that day ever coming," he said.

"Oh, but it must. And when it does you'll be so courted and flattered you'll scarcely have a glance to spare for me."

"Mary!"

"But I shall boast that I once knew the great General O'Hara and he was mighty kind to me when I was a girl and walked about Rome with me and taught me sense," she went on. "How I wish we were there again!"

"And how I wish I were twenty years younger! Where's Mephistopheles? I would be Faust, Mary."

"Oh no! I won't have that. Please stay as you are, O'Hara."

"Is that a command?"

"It is a wish," she said.

"Then I must strive to gratify it."

She thought suddenly how generous, how kind he had been to devote so much of his time to her, to give so unstintingly of his friendship and she laid her hand on his in a gesture of appreciation.

"My wish is to gratify all yours," he said, and when they parted and he made her the courtly bow which he did with such exquisite grace he said simply: "Think of that sometimes while I'm away."

8

MARY GREW ACCUSTOMED to the envy caused by
the favours Mr. Walpole showered on her family
and sometimes, on the morning following a reception or concert, she and Agnes would amuse their
father by acting impromptu sketches at breakfast.

"Such a buzz as there was at Mrs. Damer's,
Pa," Agnes would say and Mary, taking a few
mincing steps and quizzing through an imaginary
glass would speak in a passable imitation of Mr.
Gilbert's affected tone:

"My dear, have you heard the latest about Mr.
Walpole and those Berry girls? He has actually
written down some of his reminiscences for them!
In his own hand. Two copies!"

"I can scarcely believe it. Are you sure?"

Agnes was playing the part of an old dowager now with an ear trumpet.

"It's indisputable. A copy each, if you please. Inscribed 'For the amusement of Miss Berry and Miss Agnes Berry'!"

"Well, it's all of a piece, I suppose. You heard the ridiculously flattering poem he composed in their honour when they went to Strawberry Hill? *That* was run off on his press, too. You'd think them both goddesses."

"And he's christened their dog Tonton after that vile creature of the old Frenchwoman who conceived such a passion for him."

"Oh, you mean Mme. du Deffand?" The mock dowager's voice rose to a squeak.

"Yes, indeed. He had her dog over from Paris when she died."

"Ah, I remember. It bit me the only time *I* ever went to Strawberry Hill. So Miss Berry's dog is to be called Tonton, is it? Whatever next, I wonder?"

Mr. Berry had put down his paper to watch.

"Why, my dears, you should be on the stage!" he declared. "How O'Hara would laugh if he could but see you both now. Pray do write and tell him, Mary. It will divert him."

"Yes, Pa, I think I will, but there isn't time now," Mary said. "I promised Mrs. Damer a sitting this morning."

"What, is she to carve you in marble?" exclaimed Mr. Berry.

"I don't yet know what she intends, but I mustn't keep her waiting," Mary said, and she went off with the comfortable feeling that it didn't matter what people said since they were all welcomed and accepted by Mr. Walpole's relations who might well have been forgiven if they had shown some jealousy.

She felt their position in society was far more secure now they were the friends of Anne Damer and of her parents, Marshal Conway and his wife, Lady Ailesbury. She had never, in her wildest dreams, expected to be invited to stay with the Conways at Park Place but the visit had not only taken place but had been repeated, so what else could she conclude but that they had acquitted themselves well?

How fortunate it was, she reflected, that dear Pa had such wide literary interests and could talk so well and so charmingly once he was on his favourite subject, and how lucky that Mr. Walpole and Marshal Conway shared his enthusiasm.

She smiled as she thought of the three of them arguing over the merits of Pope and Dryden, the Marshal so commandingly handsome still and with such a melodious voice; Mr. Walpole stabbing in with totally unexpected and irreverent remarks, his thin shoulders shaking with laughter, and dear Pa rotund and jovial, often surprising them both with an argument that had occurred to neither.

She arrived at Mrs. Damer's studio to find her friend ready for work in a man's coat, thick woollen stockings and clumsy boots.

"I hate finery," Mrs. Damer said. "I'd never bother with it but to please my parents."

"Artists can afford to be unconventional," Mary said. "I'd love to be gifted, but I do enjoy fashion. It's fun."

"Within limits," Mrs. Damer said rather tersely

and Mary suddenly remembered she had good reason to be averse to extravagant clothes since her husband had spent a considerable fortune on his wardrobe before he shot himself.

"Did you seriously mean me to sit for you or are we just to gossip?" she asked. "I'm yours for the morning."

"I want to take a long look at you, Mary. From all angles. I want to model a bust of you and I've a particular reason for wishing to make an exact likeness."

"I've no doubt you will, but is this project more important than your others?" Mary asked.

"Without a doubt. I'm doing it for Mr. Walpole. At his special request."

"Oh!"

"You sound surprised."

"I am. Mr. Walpole has such splendid treasures that a likeness of me, no matter how superbly executed, would surely be out of place among them—just by reason of the subject, I mean."

"My dear Mary, in this instance it is the subject that counts," said Mrs. Damer firmly. "There now. You've lovely features, almost perfect symmetry and your head is set superbly. I doubt if I shall do you justice enough though I'll try. When do you move to Twickenham?"

"Next week," Mary said.

"Then we shall often meet at Strawberry," Mrs. Damer said.

Her prediction came true and one evening when they were all there Lady Ailesbury confided to Mary that she had never seen Mr. Walpole so happy.

It was so warm that they sat in the garden where the smell of syringas, honeysuckle and new-mown hay filled the air and they could see the fireworks from Ranelagh tattering the velvet of a black-black sky.

"He's always been young in heart but you and Agnes have extended his lease of summer," Lady Ailesbury said. "I'm so glad you took the house in Montpelier Row."

"It's too far off," grumbled Mr. Walpole, catching what she said.

"But we can walk to you now," Agnes said.

"It's halfway to China," he complained.

"You see how attached to you he is," whispered Lady Ailesbury.

"I'm sure he's much more attached to you and Mrs. Damer," Mary replied.

"I'm part of the furniture of his life because my mother was one of the maids of honour he loves telling you about, but his devotion to you is something quite new. It does not surprise me altogether," Lady Ailesbury went on. "Our O'Hara described you to me long ago and when we met I discovered there was no flattery in what he said."

Mary often thought of O'Hara. She missed him and stored up things to tell him when he came back. He always made life more exciting and there was no one else with whom she felt so completely at ease, so relaxed and yet so stimulated.

But even without him life was particularly pleasant just now. There was a timelessness at Strawberry and she was far from tired of it.

And then something happened which everyone took as a great joke.

One evening—it was a delicious fragrant evening with a great yellow moon—Mr. Walpole sat with Mary and Agnes looking across the lawn to the river which rippled with gold. It was an entrancing scene and they were all three silent.

Mary felt vague stirrings of emotion which she didn't understand. They were disturbing and not of a kind she had words to express. She only half listened as Mr. Walpole began talking for he only spoke, as he so often did now, on the happiness they had brought him.

"The truth is that I'm in love with you, Mary. And with you, Agnes. You are my two adorable wives and you have mellowed your peevish old husband beyond recognition."

Agnes's laugh was sweet and gentle. "What pretty things you say," she said. "I wish young men were half as gallant as you."

"Young wives with an old husband should have no concerns with young gallants," he countered.

"Well, in truth we haven't," Agnes said. "I'm more than honoured to be one of your wives so long as Mary is the other."

"Mary says nothing," he observed.

Mary did not know what to say because she had been taken so unawares. Her reply came automatically.

"Dear Mr. Walpole, this is one of your prettiest whims and I'm sure Papa will be vastly entertained and as flattered as we are," she said.

But in her inmost heart she felt a sudden distaste. She knew Mr. Walpole spoke in jest, and yet she was disturbed.

"Never mind. Nobody heard him but us," she consoled herself.

But other people did hear. The notion became Mr. Walpole's chief topic of conversation. He told everyone he was in love with the Berrys and as soon as the scandalmongers got wind of the news it spread like wildfire through the London drawing rooms and found its way to Paris and Rome and Florence.

There were men and women of the calibre of Mrs. Tristram and Mr. Gilbert everywhere and Mary found it impossible to avoid them. She was not always ready with an apt return to their pointed remarks, or to the impertinent questions mere acquaintances asked.

"I hear that Mr. Walpole now refers to Mr. Berry as 'our Papa'," a parrot-faced woman remarked to Mary one evening at a card party.

"He also calls himself Mr. Berry's son-in-law," Mary replied. "Few people appreciate the joke as Mr. Walpole's humour can be of the subtlest. He often consults Mr. Berry on literary matters so the relationship is an intellectual one. A great honour to my father, would you not agree?"

"Oh," said the woman, and she was so nonplussed she lost the trick.

But Mary's uneasiness grew day by day. Mr. Walpole was a dear, gentle, charming old man and she felt a deep affection for him, but she began to see his pronounced partiality was doing them harm.

Her father only laughed when she tried to express these fears.

"Don't distress yourself, my dear. Everyone likes you," he said indulgently.

"Not quite everyone, Pa. Some of them will never forgive us for being Mr. Walpole's favourites."

"If they envy you they might like to try our recipe and see how they like being cut off from a fortune," remarked Mr. Berry. "I doubt if Mr. Walpole would have looked at you twice if you'd been ordinary heiresses. Your misfortunes have made you extraordinary, my dear."

Mary found little comfort in this theory and when Agnes told her that Mr. Walpole was printing a catalogue of Strawberry Hill and dedicating it to them she was thoroughly disturbed.

"Aren't you pleased?" Agnes asked.

"Flattered, perhaps, but I wish he wouldn't," Mary said.

"What a glum thing you are! I suppose you see something ulterior in it? You're so prickly!"

Mary was silent. She was wondering what O'Hara would advise her to do if only she could ask him.

Suddenly the thought came: "Italy! We'll go to Italy!" It was as though he had thrown her a lifeline.

She saw Mrs. Damer next day for a final sitting and came straight out with her idea.

"Oh my God! What on earth will Mr. Walpole do without you?" exclaimed Mrs. Damer, plumping down on the steps.

"Do you think he'll mind so much?" asked Mary.

"Mind? He'll go demented! If he hadn't had your Tonton to look after the last time you were in Yorkshire I don't know what would have become of him," Mrs. Damer replied.

"Papa is very positive we should go," said Mary, though she hadn't yet mentioned the idea at home. "I'm fast losing my Italian, and we want to see as much of the world as we can while it's still possible. I daresay we may spend a year in Florence."

"A year!" echoed Mrs. Damer. "I advise you to break it to Mr. Walpole very gently then. He'll fret himself ill."

"But that would not be reasonable. A year soon passes," Mary said. "I'm deeply touched to know he thinks so highly of us but . . . "

"Of *you*, Mary," Mrs. Damer interrupted. "I know he tells everyone he's as much in love with Agnes, but the plain fact is that he's in love with *you*."

"You must be joking," Mary said, feeling more alarmed than ever.

"Indeed I am not. He thinks of nothing but pleasing you and can't bear you to be out of his sight."

"You distress me. I hope you exaggerate," said Mary, but her inside churned over and over for Mrs. Damer was confirming her worst fears.

Mrs. Damer turned back to her work, but presently she said: "He won't be the only person to miss you. I shall be utterly desolate, too."

She had only once spoken of her disastrous marriage and told Mary of the shattered hopes and crushing humiliations she had suffered as she came to know her husband's character, but Mary could easily see in this middle-aged woman the pretty and talented girl who had gone confidently into marriage with Lionel Damer and become disillusioned and miserable as his debauches and debts multiplied.

Mary never ceased to admire the way Mrs. Damer had mustered her courage when her husband shot himself, how she repaid his debts, took up her art again and made a life for herself.

"I have nothing to thank men for," she told Mary, who understood and agreed with her vehement insistence on a woman's right to liberty. She felt now that she, too, had a right to choose her future, and as soon as she got home she put her plan to Agnes.

Agnes drew a long breath. "Oh, how I'd adore to see Florence again," she said rapturously. "Pa darling, do you hear what Mary says? We're to go to Italy in the autumn."

Mr. Berry listened with growing enthusiasm, nodding his head wisely as Mary enlarged on the scheme.

"Excellent," he agreed. "Let us set about making arrangements at once."

"Straight away," Mary said, and she lost no time in setting the plan in motion. Mr. Berry dutifully signed all the letters she wrote.

"I'm very glad I thought of this," he said. "Dear me, though. What will Mr. Walpole say? He has grown so accustomed to you two running in and out."

They all agreed that it would be best to delay telling him till everything was settled as he fretted himself into a frazzle if they were away for any length of time, but it was as though he had a premonition of their tour for he never lost a chance of telling them how bad things were abroad.

"I hear all the English have left Paris. They don't think it safe to stay," he told them and he talked about riots, the mobs that roamed the streets and the attack on the Bastille.

"They have even killed the Governor," he said. "I should be greatly alarmed if any of *my* friends were to think of travelling through France while it's in such a turmoil."

"Oh, I don't think travellers unconcerned with politics would be in any danger," Mr. Berry said placidly.

"I'm thankful my dear old friend Mme. du Deffand is dead!" Mrs. Walpole exclaimed testily. "I had word this week that her nephew was dragged from his sick-bed and hanged on a lamp-post."

"Deplorable," said Mr. Berry, shaking his head.

Mary was sincerely grieved by Mr. Walpole's distress and tried her best to console him. "Many people seem to travel unscathed," she said. "I met a family only yesterday who came all through France and didn't see a sign of any disturbance."

"Then why is Richmond full of the French?" Walpole countered. "Do you think they've come to see the regatta?"

She had no answer to this but made up her mind he must soon be acquainted with their plans and steeled herself to tell him.

At first he disbelieved her, but afterwards he sat gazing at her with a piteous expression, his arguments unspoken. Then he sank his head in his hands, careless for once of displaying his swollen fingers with the great chalk-stones that made them hideous.

Agnes, sitting beside him, laid her hand gently on his arm.

"The time will soon pass," she said.

"Too soon," he groaned. "My sweet lamb, at my age a man is miserly of time. And now you are leaving me how can I joke and call you my two wives any longer? You are my children. My darling children. I love you both and that's why I plague you with my fears for your safety. Would you expect me to say nothing, loving you as I do?"

Mary had taken his snuff box to refill but she hastily replaced it on the table by his side and dropped on her knees at his feet begging him to dismiss his fears. "We shall be back with you next year and we shall be all the more cheerful and better for the change," she said.

He considered this and then replied: "No doubt you will both benefit by it and enjoy fresh scenes. If it were not for the hope of that I don't think I could bear to part with you. As it is I shan't breathe till I know you're safely in Turin."

He sighed deeply and got to his feet with difficulty and they set off with him between them on his customary tour of the house and as they went he tore Mary's heart by talking of the joy they had brought him and his desire to do something for them that would be of material help.

"Pray don't think of such things!" she cried in dismay. "We've already enjoyed so much through knowing you—please don't think of doing any more for us."

"But I do, my pet. Fate has treated you cruelly. I often dwell on it, believe me, and I shall find a way to help you."

There was a house in the grounds where Kitty Clive, the actress, had lived for the last years of her life. He led them to the window and pointed it out.

"Cliveden has been empty far too long. It would be just the place for my Berrys," he said.

He was so delighted at the idea that nothing Mary could say prevented it from running away with him. He built up a picture of Cliveden with them established there and in his mind it was already spring and the narcissi were flowering frosty white in their garden.

"I can already see our Papa strolling in the sun with his book and Tonton tumbling over himself for joy," he said.

There was no check to the torrent of ideas and the prospect of future joy was his only palliative against the pain of parting, but Mary was wretchedly uneasy about it.

"I do hope he doesn't mean it," she said, when she told Mr. Berry of the proposal that evening.

"But it would be heaven to live at Cliveden," Agnes said.

"Perhaps it would, but we'd be in a miserable position. We'd be beholden. Don't you see?"

Agnes clearly didn't. Mr. Berry doubted if anything would come of it.

"I think you should let Mr. Walpole know we couldn't accept it," Mary said. "It would be only fair to him to do so before the idea obsesses him and you could put it delicately, Pa."

"Oh no, my dear. I couldn't assume. Let's leave it in the lap of the gods."

She thought this wrong but could not prevail on him to act. It was another example of his refusal to accept responsibility and she made herself ill with anxiety over it.

"Thank God we're going away," she thought.

But Mr. Walpole's misery at their approaching separation distressed her wretchedly.

"I doubt if I shall live to see you again, my dear, sweet Mary," he said, and when she saw him hobbling painfully across the great hall supported by his servants she was overcome by pity.

"All right. We won't go. We'll stay and comfort you!"

She pressed her hands over her mouth. Otherwise the words he longed to hear would have come pouring out and they would never have got away.

9

THE BERRYS HAD scarcely settled in at Megot's Hotel when Mrs. Tristram called to see them.

"My dear Mr. Berry, how handsome your daughters look—and not a day older!" she declared.

There had been sad changes in Florence! To think dear Lord Cowper was dead since their last visit, and Sir Horace Mann, too, and so the flow of letters from that wonderful Mr. Walpole had ceased and Florence wasn't the same any more.

"The end of an epoch," she said. "We get so little news from London now," and in complete contradiction she went on to tell Mr. Berry that his daughters were talked of everywhere as the prettiest and most sensible girls to take the capital by storm for years.

"They have so many admirers—and one in particular, I'm told," she said archly.

"Pray do tell us his name for I'm sure there's no need to make a mystery of it," Mr. Berry said pleasantly.

"Oh come, Mr. Berry! I'm waiting for you to tell me!"

"I'm quite in the dark, I assure you, madam."

"How very deep you are! I'm speaking of Mr. Walpole and longing to know which of your girls has won his special approbation. Everyone knows you live much with him now."

"It's true we visit him at Strawberry Hill," Mr. Berry conceded.

"How comfortable it will be for you all when you settle at Cliveden then."

"At Cliveden? What is this about Cliveden?" Mr. Berry enquired.

"Oh, then there's no truth in the report that Mr. Walpole's given you Mrs. Clive's house? And we all thought what a splendid idea it was!"

Mrs. Tristram's shrewd eyes raked their faces and Mary felt so much dismay that she feared she showed it and said abruptly:

"I'm surprised our affairs interest people enough to call for so much as a mention."

"My dear Miss Berry, it would not be flattering to Mr. Walpole to suggest that anything concerning him lacks interest. His activities are always news to us," Mrs. Tristram said.

"But ours are not," said Mary.

"Then you don't realise how much of the light that shines on him reflects on you," responded

Mrs. Tristram, "you can't hope to remain undistinguished, even if you would."

When they were alone Mr. Berry said: "How fast news travels! Of course we can't admit it, but I've no doubt Mrs. Tristram is right and that Mr. Walpole does mean to bestow Cliveden on you."

He began to discourse on the merits of the house and on its happy atmosphere which Mr. Walpole attributed to the influence of his great friend, Mrs. Clive.

Mary countered her father's opinions with her own: Kitty Clive had not been young and she had not been dependent. She had been an actress at the top of her profession while she and Agnes subsisted on their father's annuity which would die with him. When that miserable event occurred they might go as governesses or maids for all their relations would care. To accept material help from Mr. Walpole would be to put themselves under a heavy obligation.

"And I won't be subjugated!" she exclaimed. "Do let's go and live in Pisa where we shall at least escape hearing all this gossip."

Mr. Berry agreed, but although they escaped the scandalmongers, they were the recipients of Mr. Walpole's letters which soon came pouring in by every post. These were full of his anxiety for them and his doubts of living long enough to see them again. He thought of them all the time and was having his parlour practically torn to pieces and re-made for the purpose of setting off a painting Agnes had done.

Most disturbing of all, Mary thought, were his

frequent references to Cliveden which he now spoke of as though it was actually theirs.

"When you are at Cliveden—*your* Cliveden . . ."

She could almost hear the tones of his voice and she was torn between her compassion for him and her desire to be free.

But it was spring in Italy and the air was fragrant with the scent of wild violets and warm earth and the girls were beautiful and the men so handsome, and how could she stay cool and unmoved when she was young and longed to be giddy and carefree and for once, just for once, to forget responsibility.

"How wonderful it would be to live here always!" she kept saying. "Don't let's ever go home, Pa."

"But what of Mr. Walpole? What would he say?" responded Mr. Berry.

One day they had a surprise visit from O'Hara's friend, Mr. Barnes, who had been in Rome and was going home because the news from France which was now in the grip of revolution grew more alarming daily.

"If you intend to return you should go now," he told Mr. Berry emphatically. "You may be cut off from England for years if you delay longer. Can you imagine anything worse than the King and Queen of France being held prisoners? They even talk of bringing her to trial."

"The Queen of France! It's scarcely to be credited," said Mr. Berry. "Why, we saw her in Paris on our way here—we hadn't the least trouble in getting here, you know."

"For heaven's sake don't go near Paris now,"

urged Mr. Barnes. "Avoid France at all costs, Mr. Berry."

Mr. Berry began to think they ought to go home but he still opined that the reports were exaggerated and as Mr. Barnes saw it was no use arguing with him he joined Mary at the other end of the room.

"Our friend O'Hara is in London, Miss Berry," he said, speaking with a certain tenseness that puzzled her.

"London will be the gayer then," she said. "I almost wish we were there."

She was surprised that Mr. Barnes did not respond to her cheerfulness.

"I thought you would have heard that he'd been shamefully used," he said.

"How so?"

"He has been passed over for the Governorship of Gibralter."

"Oh my God!" she exclaimed involuntarily. "He had his heart set on it."

"I know . . . "

"I can hardly bear to think how he must be suffering from this mortification," she said. "I feel almost as though the blow had been struck at us. But what is the reason for it?"

"I know of none. Lack of influence, perhaps. His record speaks for itself, but it is said in some quarters that his career is finished."

"Oh no! I shall never believe that. He needs the faith of all his friends now, Mrs. Barnes. How I wish I were at home to give him my little measure of support."

"It does me good to hear you speak so," said

Mr. Barnes. "When I saw him last he spoke so warmly of you—indeed, you were his chief topic of conversation."

She smiled. "He is my dearest friend," she said.

"May I tell him you said so?" he asked.

"Why, of course you may, but he knows it already," she said.

"It will do him good to hear it repeated."

She felt more concern than she knew how to express and after Mr. Barnes had left she could not get O'Hara out of her mind. She felt so indignant to think he had been slighted. But while she thought of O'Hara's wrongs Agnes and her father dwelt on Mr. Walpole's misery of which his letters left them in no doubt. He could not wait for them to be at Cliveden.

"Poor Mr. Walpole! We shall simply have to go home. He has been so kind to us," Agnes said.

Recollections of their evenings with him were now tinged with regret because he so clearly thought they had deserted him. But what fun it had all been! How they had laughed and questioned and begged for more of his stories.

"But I shall bore you," he temporised.

"No, no, no!"

"Well, if you insist on coining an old gentleman . . ."

"We must expect some dross! But this old gentleman's dross is gold dust!"

"Yes, we must return, if only to make it clear that we can accept no favour but his friendship," Mary thought.

They ignored all advice and went home through

France where she was more occupied with the problems in her own mind than with fears of the ruffians who roamed the streets of Paris.

In London they went straight to the house they had taken in North Audley Street. It was November and the journey from Dover in thick fog had been tiring and unpleasant.

They arrived to find one small fire flickering in the hearth and all the furniture swathed in dust sheets, but the beds were aired and it wasn't long before Mr. Berry and Agnes took their candles and departed.

Mary was in no mood for sleep. She sat on a low stool stretching her hands to the fire and watching the shadows her solitary candle cast on the walls. But the shadows changed—they played tricks. She had half heard the door open quietly, half heard voices.

Then she felt a hand on her shoulder, warm and strong.

"I knew you would come, O'Hara," she said.

She hadn't realised till then how much she had missed him and she rose and held out her hands to him.

"It's been three years," she said. "Another three. Do you realise how long we have been friends?"

"The time when we were not is out of mind, Mary. But these last years seem the longest and weariest of my life and I have nothing to show for them but stiffer limbs and a deeper scowl. I believe you are lovelier than ever and as sweet as though a crabbed thought never entered your head. I've missed you consumedly."

"And I you. Mr. Barnes gave me news of you at Pisa and I longed to be home to give you what support I could. Tell me, do things go better with you now?"

"Thank God they do. And they may improve still further. At least I have a better regiment."

"That comforts me a little."

"And your concern for me consoles me more than the highest command I could be offered!"

"How you flatter me. But in truth, would you expect a friend to be indifferent to your fortunes? I'll wager you'll attain your ambition yet, despite this setback."

"Who can tell? I trust so. But what of you? Do you stay in town for Christmas?"

"I scarcely know," she said, moving away from him. "We may be at Twickenham. Mr. Walpole wants us to live at Cliveden and he says he has it all ready for us."

"You are to be his tenants there?" O'Hara asked.

"He wishes to secure the house to Agnes and me."

"And you don't like it. I can tell by your voice."

"Indeed I don't!" she exclaimed. "I don't wish it, but how is it to be refused? Mr. Walpole has been so excessively kind to us all and having us at Cliveden is the wish of his heart."

"Having you, Mary," O'Hara said. "That's the difference."

"Don't speak my fear aloud!" she exclaimed and she began to walk agitatedly about the room.

"I would have stayed in Italy for the rest of my life to avoid this."

"Then resist it," he said.

"How? My father and Agnes welcome the idea. They cannot—will not—see what this could mean. In the general way they are glad enough to throw the weight of making a decision on me; with this they take a different view. We argued all the way home."

"If you value your independence you'll fight."

"But I must have a reason—I must have arguments."

"There's one obvious one. You will wish to marry."

"But I don't."

"Mary, think deeply. Of all the men you know is there not one you could look on as a possible husband if . . . "

"If what?"

"If he had something worthwhile to offer you?"

She sat down and supported her chin on her hands. Men! She knew dozens of them, but there wasn't one she could think of as a husband. And of the offers she had had . . . no, no!

"Haven't you some advice that doesn't depend on an if?" she asked.

"The more you accept from Mr. Walpole the stronger the bond between you becomes. It's forged of gratitude and pity on your side, I suppose."

"And a great deal of affection, too, on both sides. He wouldn't want me to be unhappy, would he?" she pleaded.

"I have the greatest respect for him, but I can't guess at his motives. Surely you don't have to make an immediate decision? I have to be away some days. If you would but delay it till I come back . . ."

"But the decision won't be mine! I've told you that Pa and Agnes wish it strongly. Point out the dangers to Papa, O'Hara. He can't see them coming from me."

"I shall do my utmost when I return," he said. "In the meantime prevaricate. You can find ways to withstand his blandishments a week or so."

"I'll do my best, but I shall depend on you to take my part," she said, putting her hand in his.

"You have reason," he replied, and she thought he was going to say something else for he looked down at her hand as though he was on the point of voicing a thought that weighed heavily with him.

The solitary candle had almost guttered out and the watchman's melancholy call told them another day had begun.

And O'Hara said nothing more.

10

THEIR SHUTTERS WERE barely down and the rooms ready before a stream of callers began and everyone seemed to know about Cliveden and took their move to it for granted.

Lady Ailesbury was one of the first and she was overjoyed because her dear Mr. Walpole's wish was at last to come true.

Mrs. Damer arrived, her pale face flushed with the pleasure of seeing them again. She took an early opportunity to tell Mary that Mr. Walpole's favourite niece, the Duchess of Gloucester, had said she was very glad her uncle had found a way of recompensing them for a small part of what they had been cheated out of.

"Oh Lord! I'm not so anxious to be recompensed!'' Mary thought in dismay and aloud she said: ''We haven't accepted yet, Anne, and I wish everyone wouldn't assume that we have.''

''It'll kill him if you refuse. Wait till you see the improvements he has made for you at Cliveden. Oh, I wish you could have seen the joy with which he greeted each one! Why, even at Strawberry everything he does is only of interest because *you* will see it.''

''We have never inspired a friendship like this in anyone before and to find that we are indispensable to Mr. Walpole's happiness quite alarms me,'' exclaimed Mary.

Mrs. Damer laughed and said: ''If I so much as dared to have a letter from you while you were away he wouldn't even listen to it! And nobody else was allowed to worry about your journey, though God knows, I'm sure I was as anxious as he.''

Mary found all this disconcerting in the extreme and she told Mrs. Damer so. ''And O'Hara was concerned, too, when I told him,'' she said. ''He called the moment we arrived.''

Mrs. Damer tapped her finger restlessly on the arm of her chair and bit her lip.

''O'Hara is very fond of you so I wish he liked me better, but he's jealous,'' she said.

''Because you and I are such good friends? Oh no, I won't have it,'' objected Mary.

''A man is often jealous of a friendship between two women if he happens to be attached to one of them,'' Mrs. Damer pointed out.

''I think you wrong him. He's far too good and true a friend to be possessive,'' Mary said. ''And besides," she added with a laugh, "I don't enquire about the company he keeps. He and I understand each other perfectly."

"I wonder if you do," said Mrs. Damer broodingly.

Mary had quickly sensed the deep sincerity underneath Anne Damer's prickly façade. The easy charm that made her mother, Lady Ailesbury, so delightful was lacking in her and it was sometimes hard to believe that she had once been the jolly little girl who was left in Mr. Walpole's care whenever her parents' duties took them from home. But Mary had struck the right note with her. They were both ambitious and they both felt themselves unfulfilled and lacked power to right the balance. This alone made for inexhaustible talk and promoted ideas that they enjoyed exchanging and enlarging on.

After all the visitors had gone Mr. Berry put an arm round each of his daughters and said contentedly:

"Well my dears, we shall soon be at Cliveden! Now that it's clear none of Mr. Walpole's relations object I'm sure my darling Mary won't be able to think of anything against it either."

"But I can and I do and I only wish I could convince you," Mary replied. "I have been right before, you will admit, Pa."

"But think of the delightful prospect before us! And I can be of use to Mr. Walpole in his literary ventures—his press and so on."

"How well you put it, Pa," said Agnes admiringly.

"And how much easier our affairs will be when

we have no rent to pay and can keep our own hens and practise a thousand economies,'' Mr. Berry continued. ''You will be in the seventh heaven organising it all, Mary.''

''I doubt it, Pa,'' said Mary.

''For once you must allow your Papa to know best,'' Mr. Berry said, and she saw it would be useless to argue but she brooded silently and quite dreaded meeting Mr. Walpole again.

But when he came she found herself transported back into the charmed life of Strawberry Hill for he brought its atmosphere with him. The meadows gilded with buttercups and fresh with diamond dew, the spreading trees, the gently flowing river, the woods and hills and all the delights of Twickenham were in his talk.

His solicitude for them and his pleasure in seeing them again were so sincere, so selfless, that she was moved almost to tears by it. He was attired as for a state visit to honour their return but she could only see him as a fragile old man hobbling into his garden in his dressing gown to feed the birds and squirrels that waited for him every morning and came swooping or scampering from the trees while he scattered food and talked to them and looked up at the sky and round at the beauty of nature, exulting in it all before he made his painful way indoors to take his own frugal breakfast in the company of his cat.

''To think you braved the horrors of France, and all on *my* account,'' he kept saying. ''I wouldn't have had you take such a risk for the world and if I'd known you were in Paris . . . ! But thank God you are safe and will soon be home at your Cliveden."

He expounded at length on the joys to be had at Twickenham but at last he said: "You mustn't think, not for a moment, that I mean to monopolise you two. I only want you to be happy, my dear lambs, and free of some of the cares you should never have had to bear."

His sincerity was unquestionable and it weakened Mary's objections so successfully that Mr. Berry refused to listen to any further arguments from her.

"Nothing can shake the Berrys from the bough," he trilled, as he tripped buoyantly about the house, and he wasn't in the least perturbed when he heard that Mr. Walpole's nephew, Lord Orford, had died, and supposed it was a happy release as the poor fellow had bouts of madness and had been a great worry to his uncle.

"But Pa, Mr. Walpole is his heir. He will be the Earl of Orford now," Mary pointed out.

"Dear me! I don't believe I shall think of him by any name other than Walpole," her father said, and at the very next meeting they discovered that congratulations on his elevation to the peerage were not acceptable.

"I don't want to be anyone but Horace Walpole! I shall never learn to sign myself Orford! I *won't* be Orford!" he declared petulantly when they called at Berkeley Square. "If anyone dares to address me as 'Your Lordship' I shall shriek!"

He was dreadfully put out.

"Just think, my dear sir, I shall be inundated

with business that I shan't understand and I'll be at the mercy of the lawyers!'' he moaned to Mr. Berry. ''I shall go quite distracted. But I shan't change my style of living to please anyone. Oh, how thankful I shall be to have you all at Cliveden!''

Mary was sorry for Mr. Walpole because he had so much to do in connection with the estate but she was glad when he saw the humorous side of his situation and wrote witty little verses about it.

Agnes sang them all round the house:

''An estate and an earldom at seventy-four!
Had I sought them or wished them, t'add one
  fear more.
That of making a countess when almost four
  score . . .''

One evening Mary went to a thé at Lady Herries'. The room was crowded, but wherever she went she found her particular bête noire, Mr. Gilbert, at her elbow trying to make conversation.

''When do you go to Cliveden, Miss Berry?'' he asked.

''When we are ready, Mr. Gilbert,'' she replied.

''What a crush there is here,'' he exclaimed testily as someone pushed him, causing him to spill his tea, which was hot. ''Dratted poison!'' he exclaimed.

''Rat poison?'' enquired Mary innocently offering him another cup. ''Have this. It's fresh and a little stronger.''

He bit his lip and forced a smile. ''I hear that Mr.

Walpole—Lord Orford, I should say—speaks of taking a wife," he said.

"You are in his confidence, I suppose?" she remarked.

"Oh, everyone speaks of it."

"Everyone repeats his verses—rather a different matter," she said.

"But he could charge the estate an extra two thousand a year for a wife," he told her.

"How interesting! I wonder you don't keep that information till you find someone who wants to know it. I do not," she replied, turning away.

She thought Mr. Gilbert's tone offensive and in a strange way almost threatening. He was watching her; she could see his reflection in one of the long glasses and noticed the look in his mean eyes.

"What a creature that Gilbert is!" she said, finding herself beside Mrs. Damer. "What an abomination with that long damp nose and those bubbles of spit on his lips. He looks as though a snail's crawled over him."

"Be careful. He's dangerous," Mrs. Damer said.

Mary laughed. "I'm not afraid of him," she said. "What harm could he do me?"

"Talk," said Mrs. Damer.

Mary thought no more about him.

Next day she woke to a sparkling world. The frost had rimed sills and railings, dead leaves caught up in old spiders' webs were silvered over and the tattered skeins hung in sparkling trails. Horses' hooves clopped sharply outside and the coachmen cocooned themselves in innumerable capes. The cold was intense.

She sat up in bed sipping her hot chocolate blissfully, savouring the full rich flavour while the maid cleared out the fireplace and set the wood crackling again. Soon Agnes came in to ask who had been at Lady Herries and what they had worn. A carriage stopped outside.

"Why, it's Mrs. Damer," Agnes said. "How early!"

"I hope nothing's wrong," said Mary.

When Mrs. Damer came in she looked worried and her greeting was almost abrupt. With a glance at the breakfast things on the table she said: "Then you haven't seen the papers, Mary?"

"Not yet. What have they to say?" Mary asked.

"This." Mrs. Damer drew a folded page from her muff and then said in an agitated voice: "No! You shan't see it. It's too horrid!"

"I hope no one's slandered *you*," Mary said anxiously. "Do show me. You came with that intention, didn't you?"

"Very well. It's better from me than from anyone else, only let me first say that not one of your friends will take notice of it."

"My friends?" Mary took the page wonderingly and spread it so that Agnes could see too. They read the piece Mrs. Damer pointed out and she watched them, pale and distressed, but they were too engrossed to notice her.

Mary had no doubt of the item's meaning and no doubt of whom it spoke. She was reading about a doting old man with a Gothic castle not far from London and of two scheming sisters who were soon to occupy a house in his grounds. The sisters depended on a father whose annuity would die with him and they had designs on the rich old man who had just been elevated to the peerage.

The story was set out with their initials and other details that made their identity clear.

"God!" cried Mary, springing out of bed. "What have we done to deserve this?"

She was white with anger.

Agnes subsided on the pillow beating the coverlet with her clenched fist.

"We're ruined!" she sobbed. "How can we go to Cliveden after this? We'll never be able to hold our heads up again!"

Mary took her by the shoulders and gave her a sharp shake. "Don't you dare say that!" she commanded. "Just let me hear you grovelling and I'll—I'll run away!"

With that she tugged at the bellrope with such fury the whole house came running and Mr. Berry thought someone had been taken ill to cause so much commotion.

"Help me to dress!" Mary ordered, thrusting all but one of the maids out of the room. "I'm going to call on Lord Orford."

"At this hour?" enquired Mr. Berry. "Whatever for?"

"To tell him we shall never live at Cliveden," Mary said.

The great house in Berkeley Square struck bleak and cold that morning. All the way there in the carriage the venomous words of the newspaper attack ran through Mary's mind.

"Mr. Walpole is bound to see how wrong it would be for us to take Cliveden now," she thought. "He'll understand. I know he will."

But the new Lord Orford looked frail and ill when he received her in a small and rather dingy parlour where he was breakfasting on tea and bread and butter.

He struggled out of his chair to greet her in spite of her entreaties that he should stay seated and he insisted on another cup being brought—the Japanese porcelain. He was drinking his tea from an ordinary china cup.

"I hate this coarse thing, but my fingers are so useless I might drop my precious porcelain," he explained. "But what do gout or china matter when you are here? Nothing matters when I see you, Mary."

Then he rambled on about the hardness of the butter in this bitter weather and his concern for his cat.

"Poor dear Muff, you are in as bad a way as your master," he said, allowing the cat to pick its way amongst the tea things on to his lap. "You have the mange, and I have the gout, but we don't care now, do we, Muff?"

He gave her no chance to tell him why she had come till everything was cleared away and then she explained about the newspaper report.

"So that's why you came so early!" he said. "I'm obliged to the paper for bringing you. A scurrilous rag, my dear. I may be feeble in my limbs, but not in my wits, Mary, and I know how to value such a report."

"Then you've seen it?" she gasped.

"Of course I have."

"Aren't you distressed by it?"

"By a vile paper? Most certainly not."

"But I am!" she exclaimed. "I'm more hurt and mortified than I can tell you. Why, it says Agnes and I are after you for what we can get! Oh Mr. Walpole, how can you bear it?"

"Easily. I'm the one who gains from our association," he chuckled.

"But don't you see we can't possibly accept Cliveden after this?" she cried. "We can't be branded as a sponging, cheating family. I won't have it said of us."

"You'll never prevent vile scribblers from taking liberties with your name," he said.

"Oh yes I will, for I won't give them cause. Pray to believe I mean what I say about Cliveden. We can never live there now."

For the first time he seemed to realise she was serious and there was a trembling, pitiful pause.

"But that's all I have to live for—to have you near me!" he burst out.

The bright eyes, so youthful in his old face, suddenly grew dim and he shielded them with a hand so distorted by gout that she had to force her pity back.

"How I wish we had stayed in Pisa! We should never have come back!" she cried.

It was as though she had struck him.

"I was touched deeper than I've ever been in my life because you left it for my sake," he said. "You will never know what misery I suffered because I was deprived of your company through those long, tedious months, but that was nothing to the agonies of knowing you were on such a perilous journey home."

He paused, and she felt that misery of his in spite of herself.

"That is over now," he went on, "and I thought, at my age, I might go on enjoying your friendship till the end of my days. Is a low scribbler to end it?"

"I am spoken of as a scheming adventuress," she said. "That is how I—how Agnes as well—appear in the eyes of the world."

"Appear? Who cares for appearances? I don't."

"But I do. Sinister motives are attributed to me and I can't bear it. How I wish no one had ever heard of me!"

"Where are your good sense and high principles now? Will you punish me because a paid hack prints a few spiteful sentences about us? Do you hold my affection for you and Agnes so cheap?"

"Oh, how can you ask that?" she cried. "You know how deeply fond of you we all are. Why, being honoured by your friendship is the one really fortunate thing in our lives."

"Well then?"

"But we value your society for what it is and not for any material reason," she said. "That is why we must decline Cliveden."

"So you'd be my friend if I were a beggar?" he parried. "I don't understand this extraordinary delicacy. You are putting yourself in the power of a newspaper."

"You can say that because you are above their power," she argued. "We are not. My father's history and the fact that every wretched detail of our misfortunes is common knowledge has always made us open to suspicion."

"You will poison the few remaining days of my life," he said.

"Pray, pray, don't speak so bitterly." Somehow she had to pacify him, to mollify him. "This isn't the end of our friendship—only of a plan," she reasoned.

"And that very plan is what keeps me alive! My dearest Mary, think again."

"But I have already thought. I *know* I'm right."

"If you can't accept for your own sake then do so for poor mine," he begged. "Think of me! You are the sweetest consolation of my old age and now that I'm pestered with the cares of a title and all the trials that go with it I am to lose the only thing I care for as well."

She kept silent, clinging to her conviction that she was doing right.

"My dearest Angel, you can sweeten my life. *Only* you. Can you truly say, knowing how pure my love for you has always been, that it goes against your principles to accept Cliveden from me?"

Mary found her resolution wavering at this appeal for it put the whole situation in a different light. She marked the sincerity of his voice and could not deny the truth of his motives. "No," she said at last, "I can't in honesty say that it goes against my principles."

She had tried so hard to live up to those principles, to cling to old-fashioned virtues: honour, truth and unselfishness and she was not being asked to relinquish them now.

Also, to refuse his wish for fear he might ask something of her in return would mean she suspected him of striking a bargain. Time and time again he had sought to show her this was not so. And she wanted to repay him for his kindness to them all. Now she saw she could do it, although it was in the last way she would have chosen.

She found her deep affection and regard for him were now balanced against something which was far less simple to define. She could only think of it as a premonition, a foreboding that had begun long ago when Mrs. Tristram's piece of malicious tittle-tattling had put her on her guard. She had realised then that it lay with her to secure the respect to which her family was entitled.

So far she had succeeded. Now she began to see that a life governed by the scandalmongers would be beneath contempt. Why should she live to please them?

"And suppose you don't come to Cliveden? What will our scribblers say then?" Mr. Walpole asked. "It's their business to ruin reputations. They'll invent another story, ten times worse than this. Take my word for it."

She felt desperately unhappy. "I've no doubt there's truth in what you say," she replied. "I will speak to my father and he shall decide."

She saw hope come back to him and found it terrible to know that it lay in her power to kindle or extinguish it. Her father, for all her talk of consulting him, was outside the picture. The decision lay with her alone.

So without sacrificing a single principle, without a scruple on her conscience, she made her choice and Kitty Clive's pretty house in the Elysian fields of Strawberry suddenly took on a different aspect. She saw it as dark and forbidding in a tangle of dead overgrowth with a river as black and heart-freezing as the Styx flowing by.

11

HOW SHE WISHED for O'Hara then! She wanted him to tell her she had done right. Could he do otherwise when he heard her account? But he was kept away by his own concerns and all was settled when he at last appeared.

For once he was more interested in his own affairs than in hers.

"I've something to tell you at last," he said. "Not the best—that is yet to come. Mary, I am appointed Lieutenant-Governor of Gibraltar!"

There was jubilation in his voice and an air of success about him that delighted her. He deserved so well!

"This is splendid news!" she exclaimed. "I am happy for you, O'Hara."

"At last, after all these years, I feel as though my wish will soon be within my grasp," he said.

"I am sure it will. You will hold the highest office before long," she said.

"My dearest Mary, do you still not know what my wish is? After all these years of close friendship have I still failed to communicate it?"

"You only told me once but of course I haven't forgotten," she said. "You wish to be Governor of Gibraltar."

"Mary!"

"Well, don't you?"

He had been sitting beside her, one arm on the back of the sofa, the other hand holding hers which she had offered in congratulation. Now his face grew dark red, he rose abruptly, strode to the window and said in an angry tone:

"Oh, don't let's speak of it!"

How touchy he was all of a sudden. She sat miserably thinking that she was of no more interest to him.

Presently he said gruffly over his shoulder: "Well, what of you? Have you fared well while I've been away?"

"No, not at all. I've done a thing I fear I shall regret."

"Then why do it?"

"Because of this."

She produced the offensive newspaper article from her desk and walked up and down the room while he read it.

"Good God!" he exclaimed. "If I could be certain of the author of this I'd call him out!"

"If you did and if you killed him you still

wouldn't solve my problem," she said.

"This is some days old. You have doubtless persuaded Mr. Walpole to withdraw his offer by now," he said.

"How I wish I had. I failed utterly."

"When we last met you'd have seized on any chance to get out of accepting!" he exclaimed. "Here you have it. This is your loophole. Don't tell me you've deliberately thrust your head into his noose!"

She was driven to Mr. Walpole's defence by this reply. "I won't hear you speak of him in that tone!" she declared angrily. "You know I'm fond of him and when I saw his distress at my refusal and heard his arguments against it I had to relent. I like, admire and honour him. How could I be so mean and paltry as to refuse when I value his friendship?"

"And what of mine? Don't you value that more than his? I begged you to wait till we met again before deciding."

"But you were absent and my hand was forced. This very article in the paper turned the scales against me."

"You could have waited," he said harshly.

"Christ! How I wish I'd stayed in Italy!" she cried. "What bliss it was with friends who weren't always flaying my emotions—who loved me undemandingly, as true friends should!"

"Very pretty, I'm sure. And with a train of oily Italians to smirk and bow and kiss your hand! I know the joys of Italian society—you needn't tell me."

"And you also know me, O'Hara, or you

should. And if I were a man, as I so often long to be, I'd know how to behave. As it is I shall simply ring the bell.''

She was white with anger and she could not keep the tremor out of her voice. He seized her hand as she reached for the rope.

''Forgive me,'' he said. ''I have been insufferable.''

''You have been—unlike yourself.'' She went to the fire and stood there holding out her hands to the blaze for her burst of indignation had drained her energy and she felt cold.

He put his hand gently on her shoulder. ''I fear for you,'' he said. ''This path you've chosen is harder than you suppose. Won't you withdraw, even now?''

She shook her head. ''It's too late,'' she said, scarcely above a whisper. She knew she had delivered herself into bondage. ''There's no escape,'' she said flatly.

''There is always a way out if you look for it!''

He laughed almost bitterly. ''It's under your nose,'' he said. ''But you can't expect me to go down on my knees to show you. I have never grovelled yet.''

And he had never looked so proud or so imposing.

''You choose to speak in riddles,'' she said, almost timidly because she felt the warm comfort of their friendship was in danger. She was almost in tears and when he spoke again it was in a much kinder tone.

''Perhaps you'll find the answer in time. This is goodbye, Mary.''

He bent and kissed her brow, a thing he had never done before.

"Think kindly of me while I am away," he said.

She did not see him again before he sailed but there was a surprise visit from Sally who came to them in a hackney carriage laden with boxes early next morning.

Agnes saw her arrive and met her in the hall. "Why, Sally, does this mean you've finished our dresses?" she asked excitedly.

"Yes, Miss Agnes," replied Sally, who looked very pale and dark round the eyes. "I've finished all my work and I'm spending the day delivering to my ladies."

Mary, on her way downstairs, noticed the strain in Sally's voice, ran the last few steps and led her into their small back parlour where a bright fire was burning.

"You're perished with the cold," she said, and she rang the bell and ordered hot chocolate and food to be brought at once and she wouldn't let Sally speak until she was rested and refreshed. Then she asked what had happened to bring her up to town so early.

"It's Rory," Sally said. "As soon as he knew General O'Hara was off to Gibraltar nothing would satisfy him but he must go as well." Her voice was thin with stress.

"But I thought he'd settled down to work in the market gardens and was doing well," Mary said. "Last time I saw him he told me his wanderings were over."

"That was then, but when his General goes

overseas he forgets everything else."

"Oh Sally, this is sad news for you!" Agnes exclaimed. "Are you to be left alone again with the children?"

"No, not this time." She pressed her hands together and then went on—"I'm to go, too, and I'm so upset and bewildered as hardly to know what I'm doing. But I've got your green silk done, Miss Mary dear, and Miss Agnes's pink. Oh, they do look so pretty and smart!"

And she suddenly burst into tears and Mary could feel the pangs that were nearly suffocating her as though they were her own. The neat, pretty cottage in its setting of market gardens, the fat, happy children with their swing in the apple tree, the excitement of making for the quality, of handling fine materials, gloating over a priceless piece of lace, feeling the sleek satin, the seductive velvets, the rustling taffetas. This was Sally's life. This—and Rory with his glinting eyes, his lilting voice, his tales of adventure. Himself.

"We shall miss you sadly, but you're doing right. I've no doubt of it," she said.

"What of the children?" Agnes asked.

"That's the worst part. They're to go to Yorkshire to my mother. Oh, they'll be well taken care of and once they settle down they'll love the farm. But it breaks my heart."

"Let us hope you won't be gone very long," Agnes said. "At least you'll know they're safe and when we visit Mrs. Seton we'll go to see the children."

"Oh, would you, Miss? Would you write and tell me how they are?"

"You may depend on us for that," Mary assured her, but although she talked encouragingly, for the rest of Sally's visit she felt dejected beyond reason, even when she counted over her many blessings.

She had no doubt that she was indispensable to her father, her sister, and to Mr. Walpole. All three made it plain to her. Yet she was so alone and there was an emptiness at the very heart of her life which she didn't know how to fill.

12

WHEN SPRING CAME the move to Cliveden was accomplished with such speed that she felt as though she had been swept up in a whirlwind and set down in a world of comfort and tranquillity which would have sucked her in completely if she allowed it to lull her sensibility.

They kept their town house in North Audley Street but this country house with its staff all ready to obey them had a seductive easiness. There were no conditions attached, yet she could never rid herself of the conviction that they existed.

They had a housekeeper, Mrs. Richardson, who was fat and efficient with a troop of rosy-faced country girls at her beck and call. Washington, the gardener, dried-up and gnome-like, with a moustache of rusty wire, deep furrows from nose to mouth and misty blue eyes looking into the distance waited for directions but made it clear he had his own ideas.

"He's even got pointed ears. I believe he's an elf," Agnes said, as they walked about the garden.

Their own William would be in charge of the stables but now there was a mount apiece for them and there were all those meadows and fields to roam and ride in. They were, as Mr. Berry aptly remarked, in clover.

"So you must admit, Mary, that Mr. Walpole was right," Agnes said as they stood by the river bank one day. "All the people we care about ignored that horrid scandal and it's died a natural death."

"But don't you think it's left a mark?" Mary asked.

"No more than a stone in the water," Agnes replied. "I shall never give it another thought and I'm perfectly certain we shall never regret making this move."

"I'm sure I hope not," Mary said. But she didn't feel sure though she freely admitted her affection for Strawberry and its owner. How could she help loving Mr. Walpole and the hours she spent with him?

He needed all the consolation she could give him, too, as the year went on.

"I hear French spoken everywhere I go," she remarked one day, "even in Twickenham."

"What can you expect with the refugees crossing the channel in their thousands?" he responded. "Oh, my dears, how thankful I am that you are safe home. If I had lost you—if you had been detained in France which you crossed at such peril to yourselves—what would have beome of me?''

"There, don't think of it now," Mary said gently.

But the news from France grew worse and the news Mr. Walpole received threw him into such a ferment that she and Agnes spent all their evenings with him that summer and dispelled his anxieties by inducing him to talk of his experiences and accompanying him through them again so they became like magical tours through time.

It was hard to believe in such idyllic surroundings, that only just across the Channel a seething volcano was on the point of erupting.

As soon as winter set in they all moved up to Town and Lord Orford, as Mr. Walpole was at last permitting his friends to call him, settled in comfortably at Berkeley Square.

The New Year came. It brought with it the news that Louis XVI had been guillotined.

In the midst of her own feeling of horror Mary was appalled to see the effect of this on her old friend. His sensitivity was even more acute than she suspected. She could feel the shudder that went through his emaciated body when he remembered his many friends in France and the thought of the peril in which they stood.

Sometimes he would sit, his thoughts far away, and then look up and say: "I begin to wonder if everything I've believed can be wrong after all, Mary."

She did her utmost to convince him otherwise

but the bewilderment of the times made the company of his friends more essential than ever before and the outbreak of war between England and France which soon followed the king's death brought new perils.

Summer came again and Mary saw with some apprehension that Lord Orford was living in dread of being left while they made their visit to Yorkshire to Mrs. Seton.

"I shan't even be able to summon up enough spirit to write to you," he said petulantly.

"But you must write," Mary said firmly. "Our Grandmother Seton depends on us to show her your letters. *Do* write."

"There's nothing pleasant to write of," he complained. "Your grandmother will be enjoying all the pleasure I lack. Let her write to me . . ."

"Oh, Lord Orford!"

"In truth, Mary, I can't write." He sounded so tetchy.

"You'll write as long as your pen has a drop of ink in its eye," she coaxed.

"Of nothing?"

She laughed. "You write nothings best of all," she said.

She coaxed, cajoled and soothed him into a good humour.

"You've such pretty eyes," he said. "Such pretty eyes."

She was looking into the distance for her thoughts had wandered off and dwelt on Sally who had written to her once or twice and told her about Gibraltar. Life there was bearable; the sun was warm, the sea—well, what a sparkle it had! There were soldiers galore and there were crowds of monkeys, too. She'd more work than she could manage making for the ladies of the garrison and there was little need now for her to keep her eye on Rory for he had his work cut out to keep his on her. But for all that the men drank and gambled more than was good for them and what wouldn't she give to be home with the children and a good cut of beef and some fresh cow's milk? If it wasn't for the war—but that would end and then they'd be home and in the meantime would Mary please send her all the news of the children?

She ended by saying that General O'Hara was splendid and the women were all wild about him.

In Yorkshire she found that Sally's brood were all in good health; they liked farm life and she could give a happy report of them. She was in the middle of writing to Sally when Mr. Berry bustled in with a newspaper.

"Mary, you know Toulon has been taken by the Allies?" he began excitedly. "Well, it says here that O'Hara's to take command!"

She felt a sudden check—a moment of fear. "Is that a good thing?" she asked.

"Excellent. Just think, he'll be able to preserve it from the revolutionaries and hold it for the Royalists. What a magnificent opportunity for him! Lord Orford will be greatly relieved to learn of this."

Her picture of O'Hara in command of the garrison at Gibraltar splintered and disintegrated. He wasn't there at all!

"I expect he's in Toulon already," Mr. Berry went on. "It's a wonderful thing to think of, Mary. They say we have command of the Mediterranean now, and of course we shall only hold Toulon in trust till the monarchy's restored."

"I wonder when that will be?" she said.

"Very soon now with the way things are shaping. We've turned the corner. How proud we're all going to be of O'Hara!"

"I was just writing to Sally," she said blankly.

"Well, don't send to Gibraltar, for heaven knows where they'll all be," Mr. Berry advised.

Mary felt so despondent and with no reason that she could explain that she had to hide her feelings from the others as best she could, especially as Lord Orford now wrote jubilant letters and evidently shared Mr. Berry's optimism.

On their first evening home in London he kept extolling O'Hara's military prowess and fitness for the post of Governor of Toulon, to which they now heard he had been appointed, but his thoughts, which he sometimes spoke aloud, disturbed her.

"I hope he won't be needed for active service—he's seen enough battles," he said.

She tried not to dwell on this aspect and to share the general optimism that grew with the hope of other towns following the example of Toulon and coming under the protection of the Allies. Perhaps the revolution would be over soon.

There was so much to do at Cliveden in the autumn that she threw herself into the delights of gardening and spent hours planting with Washington. It was a wonderful way of easing her anxiety.

"You'll wear yourself out," Lord Orford complained.

"This is the gardener's busiest time," she laughed. "Wasn't it kind of Lady Ailesbury to send us all this lavender? We'll have a hedge of it."

"You can't plant a whole coach load at once! Do get up off your knees, my pet, or you'll catch cold."

"Lord Orford! *You* to chide me when you boast of the way you go out without a hat!" she protested.

"Let Washington carry on alone now," Lord Orford said, and at Washington's jumbled mutterings he went on: "Very well, I'll send my own gardener to help you. You shall have some extra money. Oh," in exasperation, "I know you're old, but so am I!"

Washington stared into the distance as though he expected to hear a summons on a fairy horn.

Mary knew she was overtired but she couldn't tell Lord Orford she only worked so hard to keep herself from thinking of Sally and Rory—and O'Hara.

But the planting was scarcely finished and the autumn roses were still blooming when worse tidings came. Marie Antoinette had followed her husband to the scaffold. They had all dreaded and feared this to such an extent that they had not dared give tongue to their forebodings.

"The year will end even worse than it began," Lord Orford prophesied. "Oh my dears, when you think what the poor Queen suffered in that most horrible of imprisonments!"

"She was so beautiful, so dazzling, when we

saw her in Paris," Mary said. "Will there never be an end to this terror?"

They drew together round the fire, Lord Orford and Mr. Berry on either side of the chimney piece; the two girls between them. Save for the firelight the room was in darkness and they preferred it so while they spoke of the latest and most dreadful tragedy.

Mary couldn't bear to think of the guillotine and the ghastly scenes that took place there every day. She never laid her head on her pillow at night without thinking of its victims and praying for them and hoping no one she knew would ever be in danger from it.

December came. One evening when they were at a party at Mrs. Damer's Mary heard someone say Toulon had been taken.

"It can't be true!" she exclaimed, feeling as though the ground had given way.

Mrs. Damer, her face strained, said: "I expect it's a rumour. I shall not believe it till we have proof."

"It couldn't happen. Not with O'Hara in command," Mary said.

But Mrs. Damer sought out the guest who had made the remark and asked how she had come to hear of it.

"I had it from my sister who is in Italy," the woman said. "She met an English officer there who had escaped from Toulon and he told her our armies were overpowered by a huge force of the French. That's all the news I have and I only hope it's exaggerated."

"My God, if it's true what will happen to all our people there?" Mary exclaimed.

"It's best not to think," the woman replied. "I suppose it's too much to hope the French will release all our countrymen they already hold captive now they've retaken Toulon. I'm thankful I've no one dear to me in France today."

Mary was silent. She longed to be home where she could be quiet and yet she dreaded having to begin to think. She had a strange presentiment that something was about to happen which would rock her life to its foundations.

Christmas came and went and they still waited for news. The balls, receptions and dinners were gayer than ever that winter and there was an almost frantic bravado in the air. Everyone seemed to be in an excess of high spirits and Mary found herself joining in all the festivities as though each was to be the last.

She tired herself out for she couldn't rest and there was a brilliancy about her looks that made her the centre of attraction at every gathering she attended.

One night the Berrys gave a small dinner party themselves and it was so successful that the guests stayed on long after the usual time. The talk flowed. Mary and Agnes shared a talent for making people shine and their guests always went away with the feeling that they had acquitted themselves brilliantly.

Mr. Berry looked on approvingly. He was always proud of his daughters but now they were surpassing themselves—especially Mary. Dear, faithful, reliable Mary. He couldn't imagine what he would do without her.

It was almost morning when the last guest left. The servants, asleep on their feet, were sent yawning to bed; Mr. Berry went up and so did Agnes. Mary was about to follow when she heard a little whimper and Tonton was there, pawing at her, begging for a walk.

"No, Tonton. It's much too late, and I'm too tired," she said.

But Tonton continued to plead and run to the door and back so at last she relented. The dog always ran to the corner and bounded back when she clapped her hands and he had capered back twice and she had coaxed him in and was about to shut the door when a man came hurrying along the street.

She thought there was something familiar about his walk. He stopped on the opposite side, and then crossed over.

"Miss Berry?"

With a shock she recognised Mr. Barnes. He stood hesitantly at the foot of the steps.

"Mr. Barnes! Pray do come in," she said.

"I would have passed on if the door hadn't been open. This is such an unearthly hour!"

"Oh, pray come in! I'm very glad indeed to see you. You were at Toulon? Come to the fireside and let me give you some wine. You look exhausted."

He must have news—why didn't he say something? Surely he knew what she was longing to hear. "O'Hara. Where is he?"

She poured the madeira with a hand that shook and he took the glass and drank it at a gulp. His clothes were mud-stained and his face streaked with grime as though he had been riding fast and long. She made him sit down. She stirred the fire to a blaze.

"What news?" she asked, pressing her hands together.

"Bad," he said. "We couldn't hold against the French. Oh, Miss Berry, it was terrible—everything went against us. The town had been in a state of siege since August and the French brought up huge reinforcements lately. We were outnumbered—and outwitted."

"And O'Hara? Has he come with you?" she managed to ask.

"I fear not."

"Is he—dead?" she asked.

Why didn't he tell her? It was terrible, the time that went by before his answer came. She was frozen, leaning against the table. A cinder fell from the fire and a few sparks flew up.

"Taken prisoner," he said.

At first she felt relieved. She was in pain as though the cold had paralysed her and now life was beginning to come back and every atom of her body hurt as her blood began to flow swift and hot.

Barnes was exhausted. He was drooping forward in his seat, his eyes closing, muscles twitching. His empty glass slipped from his hand to the floor.

She had to know the rest. She took him by the

shoulders and shook him.

"What will happen to him—to O'Hara?" she demanded.

"It's said we killed one of their deputies. They will be revenged."

"The guillotine?"

"I fear it . . ."

His eyes closed again and he sank into a heavy sleep. She put a cushion under his head just as she always did for her father, but it was an automatic action without thought.

And then the revelation came. It was as though a flash of lightning ripped through the room, through her heart and her brain and there was an overpowering surge of sound as thought the world had burst into song and in the midst of it all she heard her own voice.

"O'Hara!" she cried. "God have mercy, I'm in love with him!"

Exultation filled her and for a moment it overcame her madly beating heart and the throbbing pain that filled every part of her and when it was over she knew that at last she was alive.

And far away, like a distant echo, there was the roll of drums, the noise of the tumbrils clattering through those squalid Paris streets and the sickening crash of the guillotine. She gripped her throat with both hands, her mouth was dry and her voice throttled.

Then she seized a wrap from the settle in the hall, let herself out of the house into a dark and misty morning and began to run, stumbling over the cobbles in her satin shoes, the end of her shawl trailing in the mire, her hair getting wet with the drizzle and falling out of curl.

Early morning workers turned to stare. Porters with baskets on their heads, women from the outskirts of town with their barrows of vegetables for market, a sweep with a tribe of ragged workhouse children.

She took no heed of any of them. They didn't exist. Only O'Hara was alive that morning, no more the comfortable friend of her youth but the man she suddenly loved.

She reached Anne Damer's house and stumbled to the door surprising a raw-faced girl who was scrubbing the steps. She said she must see her mistress immediately and a manservant appeared and she found herself in the hall waiting while the staff whispered together and gave her curious looks.

But at last Mrs. Damer peered over the banisters and when she saw Mary she came running downstairs and took her into the room she used as a study.

The news of O'Hara's capture shocked her. She was appalled, horrified.

"But you shouldn't have come so early," she protested. "You're exhausted after last night and running through the streets in the mist is enough to give you your death!"

"You are the only person I can talk to," cried Mary. "Don't you see why I ran out as I did! I'm in love with the man! I can't describe what happened when I heard this news from Mr. Barnes. I only know I love O'Hara with all my heart and I didn't realise it till I heard he's in danger. Who else on earth can I tell that to but you?''

Mrs. Damer didn't reply at once. She had her own problem to resolve for her devotion to Mary had become the most important thing in her life and she thought of their friendship as a compensation for her unhappy marriage and for the slights and humiliations she had suffered since. There were so few people who liked her but with Mary she felt her cold, prisoning inhibitions melt away. The hours they spent together talking of their ambitions and interests were her greatest delight, her nearest approach to happiness.

Mary's confession meant the end of this exclusiveness, no matter what happened to O'Hara. All Mary's thoughts, hopes and fears would now be centred on him. But, through the intensity of her own feelings, she was able to realise and understand what Mary's must be and she knew her own salvation lay in generosity.

"What can I do to help you?" she asked. "I'll do anything that will be of service to either of you.''

"You're helping already," Mary said. "There's no one else I could open my heart to and I believe you admire O'Hara even though you disagree with him on so many things.''

"I do indeed admire him, and I like him," Mrs. Damer said. "Perhaps in the future he will learn to distrust me less and like me a little more.''

She sat ruminating for a little while and then went on: "When I think of all the men I know O'Hara is the only one I would choose as a husband for you, Mary. I know he has the greatest affection for you and if he has never confessed to loving you it is because he had no hope you would return his feelings.''

"But to discover this now! He's in mortal danger, and how am I to live now knowing from hour to hour if they have killed him? Life will be unliveable!''

"No. It will be painful but you've sense and fortitude enough to bear it. If the worst happens, which God send it never will, you'll still be the better for having realised your feelings. If he loves you, as I feel sure he does, the thought of you will solace him so all your thoughts and prayers will comfort him, no matter where they may be.''

"I wish I had faith enough to believe my thoughts might reach him.''

Remembering O'Hara's plight she began to cry and to rock herself to and fro in an agony of fear. She remembered the Paris streets and the atrocious faces of the people who infested them and she thought of Lord Orford's fear and trembles and forebodings.

Mrs. Damer guessed what was passing through her mind and tried to mitigate her fears and inspire her to hope he had at least a chance of survival.

Her good sense had its effect at last and when she had persuaded Mary that a dread of defeat could, at the least, be harmful, she felt considerably better herself.

It was still early when she ordered her carriage and took Mary back to North Audley Street where they found Mr. Barnes still asleep by the fire which was now quite cold.

Neither Agnes nor Mr. Berry were stirring so nobody knew what had happened.

"I'll sit here till Mr. Barnes wakes," Mrs. Damer said, "but you must have some rest or you'll be fit for nothing."

Mary was so physically and emotionally exhausted by this time that she didn't argue and she had no sooner laid down on her bed and pulled up the covers than she was fast asleep.

13

NEXT DAY, WITH Anne Damer at her side, Mary listened to all the information Mr. Barnes could give them. They had been outdone by brilliant strategy and O'Hara had been captured in a gallant attempt to repulse an attack on the battery he had captured from the French.

"The fighting went on for seven long hours, Miss Berry. God knows how many of our men were killed. We shall learn more as time goes on."

She knew he was sparing her graphic pictures of the ghastly battle scenes and she could not bear to think of them—the salvoes of red-hot balls setting tents alight, the rearing, screaming horses, the howls of the wounded, the desperate confusion.

"We must try not to dwell on the dark side,

Mary," Mrs. Damer said.

Mary found this easier said than done and a few days later when she was driving down St James's Street with Agnes they were hemmed in by a crowd that prevented the traffic moving.

"What's happening?" she asked.

"I feel sure it's something horrid," Agnes said and she called out to William to ask him to turn off somewhere.

" 'Fraid I can't, Miss. Road's thick behind us. We'll have to stay till the crowd clears," he said.

"What's keeping us?" Agnes had to shout to make herself heard above the hubbub.

"They've set a pillory up down the bottom there."

"Oh Lord!" said Agnes, sinking back on the seat.

Mary felt herself turning green. The crowd was separating to allow barrows full of refuse to be pushed through. A truckload of stinking fish halted beside their carriage.

"I shall be sick. Let's get out and make our way back to Lady Herries, Agnes," she said. The horses were growing restive as she called out their intention to William.

"I don't advise it, Miss. You'd best wait here," he said.

"Come for us as soon as you can," Mary replied, managing to open the door a fraction so that they both had to squeeze their way out. Clinging to each other they turned to make their way back but it was impossible to resist the oncoming rush and they were borne down the street past their own carriage, their feet not touching the ground.

Mary's dress was torn, Agnes's hat was wrenched from her head and she lost a shoe. But at last they came to a halt against a solid wall of human backs. A woman turned her head and swore at them because she had been pushed and then, noticing the quality of their clothes, she said mockingly: "Oh, make way for the ladies. Let the gentry have front seats!"

They were hustled to the front, their protests unheard in the noise.

"Look up then, lady," said a man, squinting into Mary's face and half suffocating her with his stinking breath. "Have a throw, my love. What's the matter, then? He ain't your husband, eh?"

She shook her head and clung to Agnes and then she looked at the pillory. What she saw filled her with such an indescribable mixture of disgust and indignation that she stood rigid for a moment. But for a faint, twitching movement, she would scarcely have believed anyone was there; the whole instrument was plastered with the obscene and suffocating muck which had landed on it. There was no sign of a human face. Suddenly the ghastly degradation of the victim came home to her with such violence that she began to scream in the voiceless frenzy of a nightmare.

The strength went out of her legs and she would have fallen if someone hadn't caught her. She didn't know who it was and she never remembered being carried back to Lady Herries' where she recovered consciousness a long time afterwards and heard that William had managed to get help and Lady Herries had sent her servants searching and had rescued them both.

"It was the people in the crowd—more like savages than people," she whispered. "How can men and women be so vile?"

To herself she thought: "That's how the people look who gather round the guillotine. That's hatred and cruelty in the flesh. Oh God, pray keep O'Hara safe."

But there were times when she almost forgot his danger in her recollections of him. Scenes, conjured up by a single word, would flash into her mind complete and vivid. Rome—and there he was laughing to see three hundred beggars trailing behind the German Emperor who had thoughtlessly tossed down a few sequins; St. Peter's—and they were in the piazza setting their watches. Nine o'clock. Suddenly the whole church was a blaze of light from the top of the cross to the extremes of the colonnades. Terni—the cascade where they had watched the water foaming into a mist and marvelled at the rainbows.

What a spontaneous, joyful friendship it had been; how wonderful to be able to talk so freely, to laugh and quarrel, agree and argue and always to end with so much liking. She had never felt so gloriously uninhibited with anyone. And yet she had never discerned the husband she wanted in the man who was so often at her side. It had taken fear of death to illuminate him.

She began to lead a secret life. She explored every moment they had spent together, recalled every word he had said to her, and often looks that had crossed his face at things she had told him, his impatient exclamations as she spoke of people she had met and what they had said to her took on a meaning she had missed at the time. He had often watched her broodingly as though there was much he wanted to say.

"But if he cared for me why didn't he say when he was here before Christmas?" she asked Mrs. Damer.

"He had nothing to offer you then and wouldn't risk a rebuff, I think. He has always seen you in brilliant company outshining everyone. It takes courage to propose. He has been on active service all of his life and has no settled home, remember."

"I would go anywhere . . ."

"But did you ever give him a crumb of encouragement?"

"Never. But I didn't think then. Oh, it was so different!"

And suddenly she saw the real obstacle. Cliveden. O'Hara was waiting for a post when she came home from Italy and when he secured it and came to tell her he was appointed Lieutenant-Governor of Gibraltar it was with the certainty that she would have refused Lord Orford's offer and would be free to listen to him. She remembered the disillusionment in his face, his sudden anger, his concern for what she had done and his weary despair when he took leave of her.

"I knew I'd taken the wrong road. Oh God, what a fool I've been!" she cried.

She could blame no one but herself. Lord Orford's motives were purely altruistic, O'Hara could not think them otherwise, but he knew that her deep sense of responsibility, her gratitude and her affection would enslave her.

"He is the only man for me," she confided to Mrs. Damer. "Married we could make such a life as neither of us ever dreamed of! Oh, I feel there are depths in me that will never be sounded, except by him!"

New worlds opened before her at the thought; if his life were only spared she saw the possibility of achieving all she most desired. She forgot Anne Damer in her ecstasy till her friend's voice, flat and plaintive, came through from her own unhappy world.

"I shall be forgotten," she said.

"Oh no, indeed you won't," said Mary, with heartfelt conviction. "O'Hara and I will include you in our happiness—we shall include everyone we love."

Between ecstasy and torment, high hope and clutching fear, time passed.

O'Hara was a prisoner in the Luxembourg. When this news came she went down on her knees in thanks, but the next moment she was white with dread of the guillotine. She managed to keep her anguish from her father and Agnes but she sometimes thought it strange they could live so close and be so unaware of her feelings.

"I'm sure I should know if Agnes fell in love," she thought.

But Agnes hadn't an inkling of her feelings though O'Hara's name was often mentioned. Mr. Berry was concerned for him. So was Lord Orford. And because she had learned to hide her feelings so well she surprised herself by speaking of him, too, with the same amount of concern as they did, but with no more.

She found managing the garden at Cliveden was her best charm against anxiety. When she was planning and planting and insisting that Washington should give her the hoe and let her get on with it she felt a wonderful sense of calm.

"You'll get one of your 'eads," he muttered sourly.

It was true she had been suffering from more headaches than usual and although she knew what caused them everyone else insisted that it was because she did too much. They didn't realise how much physical exercise helped.

"I don't think I shall, Washington," she said.

The gardener moved off, grousing to himself audibly. "Thinks she knows best—thinks I can't tell her. Her 'ead'll kill her come nightfall."

If Washington was concerned with her health Mrs. Damer was far more so.

"Will you ever think of yourself?" she often asked, for she saw that Mary was spending herself in the service of others. She couldn't do enough for her father and Agnes and she cheerfully devoted hours to Lord Orford every day and in the evenings she had only to say a word to set him talking and he would soon be in full spate as he recalled delicious bygone scandals and indiscretions.

One morning, as she sat writing in the breakfast room, Mr. Berry came in bursting with news.

"I heard something I think you should know last night, Mary," he said.

"Oh yes, Pa," she said absent-mindedly, for she

was amusing herself in concocting a play and interruptions were not welcome.

"When I called in at my club a person I don't know very well buttonholed me and begged to congratulate me on your forthcoming marriage!"

"Heavens, who to?" she asked, still only half 'attending.

"Can't you guess? To Lord Orford, my dear."

She flung down her pen and all her fictitious characters fled.

"Good God!" she exclaimed.

"Now don't get into a pet," said Mr. Berry hastily. "I told the fellow he was wrong, but not before I'd found out how the rumour started. It appears that a certain Duchess, closely related to Lord Orford, actually asked him outright if he meant to marry you."

"That anyone should dare put such a question!" She began to tear up a discarded page of her manuscript, folding and rending it into pieces to vent her feelings. "Duchess or no Duchess, has she no delicacy—no respect for his feelings?" she demanded.

"My dear, you do not enquire what he replied," her father reminded her.

"It makes no difference to me."

"But hear it for interest's sake. Lord Orford is said to have answered: 'That shall be as Miss Berry wishes.' Only think of that, Mary."

She did think; her brow cleared and her face resumed its gentle expression as all her affection for Lord Orford welled up.

"Oh Pa, how gallant he is!" she exclaimed. "I

shall love him all the more for that retort." She
smiled as she envisaged the scene for she could
hear his tone, see his enigmatic expression and
imagine his glee as he baited his questioner. "I'm
convinced he enjoys teasing people who pester
him with nonsense," she said. "As if he would
think of proposing to me!"

"It isn't so unlikely. He may well be thinking of
it," Mr. Berry observed.

"Why Pa, how can you imagine such a thing?"

"It would be a great honour to be the Countess
of Orford," replied Mr. Berry, walking up and
down the room with his hands tucked under his
coat tails. "Just consider who he is—think of his
place in society. You would be the mistress of
Strawberry Hill! Your position would be assured
and your future provided for. *I* can do nothing in
that line, my dear."

She turned pale and a feeling of near panic began
to flutter in her inside.

"I couldn't bear it," she said, in great agitation.
"You're not trying to persuade me, are you?"

"Oh my dear, dear child, of course I'm not,"
exclaimed Mr. Berry, taking her in his arms and
patting her shoulder. "I would be the last one to
persuade you to do anything your heart's not set
on. I only want to point out the advantages so that
you may think them over. After all, you *are* very
fond of Lord Orford."

After a long pause she said decidedly: "Yes, Pa,
I am fond of him. There's no doubt about that."

Mr. Berry smiled contentedly, kissed her and
wandered off to the vegetable garden, humming a

tune to himself as he went.

Mary sat down at her desk again, but not to write. She was much disturbed, despite the humour she could see in the event, and she forced herself to think deeply. At length she decided it was her duty to make her wishes clear to Lord Orford in case he did make a declaration. She must save him from that at all costs.

Her opportunity came soon afterwards as they strolled under the acacia trees when the sun was setting.

"What a perfect evening, and how fortunate we are to enjoy it in each other's society!" she said. "We live so close it's as though we share the same roof and we enjoy so much together. I don't think we could be brought closer together by any other connection."

"Don't you, my sweet lamb?"

"I'm sure of it. And since we're as free as air our affection has room to grow, as affection always does when it's freely given."

They walked on a few paces and then she saw a peony newly staked. "Really, Lord Orford, your gardener must take some advice from Washington! He's strangling this plant—it can't breathe," she said, and she stooped to untie it and set about loosening the raffia so that she should not see the expression on his face as he leaned on his stick watching her.

His silence was pitiful, but when she looked up his emotions were serenely masked and he said calmly: "My dearest Mary, I understand you perfectly."

"We understand each other," she said. "I have been told how you replied to a certain impertinent question and I only wish I were as quick in repartee as you."

"Then you approve my answer?" he asked.

"It was perfect. It has mystified her, flattered me, and left *us* just as we are and always shall be—the best and truest of friends."

He sighed. "You spend so much of your precious time with me that I fear I must sometimes bore you," he said.

"Never. While there's no restraint on me the time I spend with you is pure pleasure—and it always will be. I promise. Does that content you?"

"It gives me inexpressible happiness," he said after a pause. Then he added: "And Mary, pray laugh at those who would make you my countess. You are the most precious thing in my life and I am too grateful for my good fortune to put it in risk by asking for more."

She felt too full to respond. Her relief was mixed with sadness for they had walked into the shadow of the house and it felt chill on them. She felt that sudden, hopeless emptiness. Things, possessions, what were they without people—without children?

But she couldn't tell him of her feelings—of O'Hara. She could not hurt him so much. Not then.

14

IN THE AFTERNOONS she often went with the others to call on their friends but sometimes she preferred to roam in the meadow that spilled down to the river and watch the boats go by.

One day she was picking wild flowers by the water's edge. It was showery, with intervals when the sky cleared completely, then, in no time, the clouds would come scurrying up. She gathered a great sheaf of varied grasses for Agnes to paint and was halfway back to the house when the rain came down.

She had to run for shelter head down and as she reached the door she heard footsteps behind her and turned to see a woman in a ragged, bedraggled gown stumbling towards her. She was so wild-looking with her haggard face and tumbled hair that Mary took her for a vagrant who had been sleeping in a haystack.

"Miss Mary, don't you know me?" the woman gasped as she was on the point of slamming the door.

"Sally!" she cried.

Sally. She was a skeleton of her old self. She was trying to speak, but her voice was only a croak.

"I was at Toulon," she said, and she fell in a dead faint across the threshold.

Mary shouted for help and Mrs. Richardson came and threw up her hands in dismay.

"Some beggar I suppose," she said. "William shall carry her to the kitchen."

"No, Mrs. Richardson," said Mary, who was kneeling on the doormat cradling Sally in her arms, "this is our own Sally who you've often heard us speak of and God only knows what she has been through."

Mrs. Richardson looked again and shivered. Then she squared her shoulders. "To bed," she said and she called William and a kitchen maid and they lifted Sally and carried her gently upstairs to the guest room with Mrs. Richardson tutting because her muddy gown soiled the counterpane. But when she saw that Sally's shoes had worn through she fetched warm water and set about bathing her feet which were sore and bleeding.

"Poor soul," she murmured. "Poor, dear soul. You always said she was plump and pretty, Miss Berry."

"She was once," Mary said.

"She's been tramping the roads. Look! Her pet-ticoats are in tatters—and her poor feet!"

"She said she was at Toulon as she fell."

"Then she'll have seen terrible things. I believe she's asleep now. Best to leave her, best to let her sleep as long as she can. We'll lay warm flannel over her chest and cover her up. Ah, the dear."

Mrs. Richardson was looking at Sally as though she might have been her own child.

Mary spent the night at her bedside and Sally didn't wake till the sun was up next morning and was so weak they all begged her to drink the warm milk Mrs. Richardson brought and to wait till she was more recovered before she tried to tell them anything.

Even when she was stronger and able to speak Mary spared her questions although she was burn-ing with anxiety for news. In the end she had to piece the story together herself for she never got a continuous and coherent account of it. Often Sally would recount an incident and then burst into a passion of tears and beg to know what was to become of her and what of the children and where were they?

"They're safe in Yorkshire and long to see you," Mary assured her, but Sally only wept more bit-terly.

"They'll never see their father again," she sobbed. "He's killed. I'll never see him again—never in this world!" And her tears flowed and she clutched Mary's arm with her thin hands and kept saying Rory's name over and over again and Mary tried to comfort her by talking of the children for whose sake she must live, but all the time her heart was crying out for O'Hara.

Sally's recovery was slow but with Mary's devoted nursing she gradually regained strength though when she thought of Toulon she would cringe and shudder and look as wild as though she had woken from a nightmare.

"We weren't there any time—only the month," she told Mary one day. "November! I shan't forget that. We heard it was all to be easy when we left Gibraltar—the General told Rory so himself."

Mary's heart missed a beat for Sally had never mentioned O'Hara till now.

"Yes, it was all jubilation when he was made Governor because he thought the Allies were united," Sally went on. "Oh God! He soon found they were daggers drawn. They didn't care for us, I can tell you. And there were so few to fight the French, allies and all, if you can call 'em allies."

"So the position wasn't what the General had been led to expect?" Mary asked.

"It was a proper mess from all I saw and heard. The General was taken in the same skirmish as my Rory was killed. I wanted to die that day."

Sally began to talk of her terror when the full weight of the onslaught came and of how she had stayed behind when the evacuation of the town began. She couldn't believe Rory was dead, not though some of his comrades who escaped told her so and begged her to fly with them. So while the inhabitants streamed down to the harbour in their thousands to be carried to safety in the ships she stood in the street clinging to a lamp-post, waiting for him.

And there were terrible explosions as some of the warships were blown up and the smoke and screams and smell of gunpowder made her think she was in hell.

Too late she realised she was stranded and she knew that much as she wished herself dead she must try to escape for the sake of her children. She didn't know which way to turn so she just knelt down in the road and prayed the way her mother taught her when she was a little girl and the next thing a man grabbed her by the hand and dragged her up so she was running with him and he gripping her arm and forcing her on though she could have dropped.

At the harbour the noise and confusion terrified her and the man never said a word. There was a small boat lying under the wall, a little cockleshell thing, and he helped her in and got in after her and pushed off, but there wasn't an oar. She said it was strange how he didn't curse or swear. She couldn't get a proper look at him in the dark but there were gleams of light and from what she could make out his complexion was dark and his eyes deep set.

She huddled in the boat thinking they must be captured but he took off his coat and his boots and gave her them to hold and then he dipped his hand in the water and made the sign of the cross and he just slipped over the side and the next thing he was swimming and pulling the boat with him.

She thought he swam a long way, a mile perhaps. He was making for another boat, further out, and at last they reached it and were taken on board. She thought the sailors were fishermen but there were several who were not the same kind at all. They treated her courteously and when morning came she saw they had sailed a long way from Toulon. She believed the sailors were Italians and realised her rescuer and the other passengers must be priests escaping from the fury of the Jacobins.

She never heard the name of her rescuer.

"But I shall never forget him," she told Mary. "He understood English and I told him all that had happened, and when we put in at Nice my gentleman and his friends were going to some monastery and would you believe it—they emptied their pockets and made me take all their money! But I didn't know where to go so they left me at a convent with the nuns."

It was through the good offices of these nuns that Sally was able to work her way to Antwerp with an English lady who wanted help with her two small children. The journey was slow and the lady hard to please but they reached the coast at last and there they parted for her employer was to stay at Antwerp.

Sally got a passage to England but the crossing was rough and she was ill. She remembered a woman offering her some brandy and after that she slept and didn't wake till after they berthed. It was then she found all her money had been stolen and she had no means to get home.

"Sometimes I'd get a lift on a cart but mostly I'd to walk," she said. "I looked a scarecrow and folk slammed their doors on me if I begged a drink of water or a crust. But I got to London and to North Audley Street and oh, Miss Berry, when I saw your house all shuttered and the knocker off the door I sat down on the step and cried."

"Thank God you are safe home now," Mary said.

If only O'Hara could be safe, too. In all Sally's story there had been so little she could learn of him.

"If my chance ever comes, if we can only meet again, I shall have nothing else in the world to wish for," she told Mrs. Damer.

"I only pray that you'll take your chance when it comes and not let it go," Mrs. Damer replied.

"How can you doubt it?" Mary exclaimed.

"Because I know your character, my dear."

"You can have no idea of my feelings then," Mary said.

"Indeed I have. But I don't think you realise the obstacles in your way," Mr. Damer warned. "Mr. Berry and Agnes will almost expire at the thought of your leaving them, but they can be managed. It's the reaction of Lord Orford that I dread most of all."

"I've thought about that, too. But he likes O'Hara," Mary said.

"He likes him as he is, but he won't like him as your prospective husband. He'll hate the man who takes you away from him," Mrs. Damer said. "Lord Orford loves you as he never loved anyone else in his life. If O'Hara returns—when he returns—all I ask is that you will let me serve you both in any way that will help. For you will need help, Mary."

"I'm more grateful than I can say. I know I can always rely on you, as you can on me," Mary said, and then she was silent for a long time.

At last she said: "I don't have to face this problem while O'Hara is captive. When he is free I pray I shall find the resolution to solve it without hurting anyone. I wouldn't grieve Lord Orford for the whole world."

"Not for O'Hara?" asked Mrs. Damer, smiling.

"For O'Hara? He's much more than the world," Mary said.

15

BUT PRISONERS-OF-WAR were not expected to fare
better than the English civilians who were clapped
in gaol by the French when the Allies took Toulon
and were still kept there after it fell.

Nothing Mary heard calmed her fears and she
had additional cause for regret when the Governor
of Gibraltar died for the post would undoubtedly
have gone to O'Hara if he had been free.

"Poor O'Hara! He always seems to miss his
chances," Mr. Berry remarked, holding his port
up to the light to admire the colour.

"Such a pity," said Agnes.

Although they both deplored his ill-luck they
looked so annoyingly comfortable while they did
so that Mary flared up.

"It's hardly his fault!" she exclaimed hotly.

Mr. Berry looked surprised. "Of course it isn't, my dear. I never said it was," he said.

"At least they haven't chopped his head off and I don't see how they can now as we didn't kill their wretched deputy after all," said Agnes. "Mr. Barnes was quite wrong about that. But of course there's no knowing.

"Oh Agnes!" cried Mary, and she ran out of the room and into the garden where she made a fierce onslaught on the weeds.

That evening she had one of her headaches and she could not stir from her room for the next few days. There was no one she could talk to. Mrs. Damer was at Park Place for Marshal Conway was dying and her mother needed her. Lady Ailesbury was beside herself with grief for her happy marriage had lasted nearly fifty years and she clung to her daughter for support.

Lord Orford bore the loss of his cousin with surprising equanimity. His affection for Conway had been lifelong and his devotion selfless so his relations always feared such a blow would be disastrous but with Mary always at hand to cheer him he appeared to be relatively unmoved. But he fretted when she had a headache or looked pale and he now became seriously concerned about her.

"My dearest dear, you should take five grains of James's powder," he advised. "It would put you right."

"But I've taken it and I still feel seedy," Mary replied.

"I think she needs a change," suggested Mr. Berry, who was itching to go away himself. "The summer has been exhaustingly hot. I'm sure if we were to go to Cheltenham and take the waters she would soon improve.''

Lord Orford couldn't bear the thought—he didn't know how he was to pass his evenings—but he upheld Mr. Berry's proposal for all that.

"I can't have my dearest looking so pale," he said.

The family set out for Cheltenham in August and they had only just turned out of their gate when Mrs. Damer's carriage drew up beside theirs. She leaned out of the window excitedly.

"O'Hara's free!" she cried.

Mary gasped and gripped her hands together pressing them against her heart. Mrs. Damer's eyes were fixed on her but as her father and Agnes were asking questions they didn't notice her agitation.

"I only know that he's exchanged for General Rochambeau and we may expect him any day now for he's sure to come to us at Park Place," Mrs. Damer replied in answer to their chorus.

"How I wish we weren't going away!" Mary exclaimed.

Mrs. Damer's look was full of compassion. "The change will do you good," she said. "I must tell Lord Orford the news and shall spend the night here. My mother wishes it since she knows how he hates the first day of your absence."

When they separated and were on the road Mr. Berry said: "Well, well, how glad poor O'Hara will be to get home, and I've no doubt the Frenchman won't be sorry either."

"I'll warrant Rochambeau hasn't suffered in our

hands as you may be sure O'Hara has in theirs with the threat of the guillotine hanging over him so long," Mary returned.

"You seem to get very heated these days, my dear," remarked Mr. Berry. "Your nerves must be very delicate. You concern yourself too much with other people's feelings and I think your own should be enough to deal with."

He opened his book and Mary leaned back and closed her eyes. Mrs. Damer's news had thrown her into such a ferment of excitement that she scarcely knew what to do with herself. After all her longing to see O'Hara she was now almost frightened at the prospect of meeting him. So many conflicting ideas beset her. Suppose he no longer liked her? It was disturbing to realise that her idea of his loving her might be nothing more than a projection of her own desire. Why should he be in love with her, after all? It didn't follow that he was simply because she had toppled so tardily into love with him.

"I wonder if he'll be different?" Agnes's voice broke in on her thoughts and did nothing to soothe her. "Being in prison so long may have changed him. He's bound to have altered. I hope he's still got his teeth."

"Oh, you're impossible!" exclaimed Mary. "How can you be so heartless?"

Agnes looked surprised and rather hurt. "It's very natural to wonder how he'll be, for he isn't getting younger, Mary. Of course, Lord Orford has still got *his* teeth, but I doubt if I'll have mine if I live as long as either of them."

"Will you please stop talking about teeth?" said Mary tensely, and she closed her eyes again.

"I won't think of such things," she told herself. "I love him and nothing will alter that, no matter if he looks as old as Methuselah and as ugly as sin—which he never could. Oh, if we could only be together for a few hours so all this time would melt!"

Her impatience was so acute that she could only bear it by reminding herself to be thankful because he had been spared.

If Anne were here I could bear the suspense better—if I only had someone to talk to!" she thought.

She exerted all her will-power to hide her feelings and managed so successfully that when they settled in at Cheltenham Mr. Berry was pleased to see that she had recovered her equanimity and was as thoughtful for his comfort as ever. His favorite snuff was always to hand, and so was his favourite wine. Mary was a remarkable manager!

They sampled all the attractions of Cheltenham, met many of their acquaintances doing the same and had never a moment to spare. One day they saw some muslin in a shop window which Agnes admired. She was sure that Sally, who was back in her Hammersmith cottage after recuperating in Yorkshire, would be able to concoct a most becoming gown from it.

"She has such ideas!" Agnes said. "Only I wonder if I really want it?"

"Only you can decide that," said Mary.

"Well, what do you think?"

"I think you should make up your mind without my opinion," replied Mary. "I agree it's very pretty."

"Then I shall have it," said Agnes. "I'll go straight away and buy it."

Mary was thankful Agnes didn't insist on her going too and as soon as she was alone she sat down to write to Mrs. Damer. She was in the mood to pour her heart out and she had to be alone to do it even though it was only on paper.

She had scarcely begun when a knock came at the door and the servant said there was a gentleman to see Mr. Berry.

"Say that Mr. Berry is out walking and will be back in an hour," Mary replied without looking up. Her pen was flying over the page. The servant had neglected to shut the door and she meant to get up and close it the minute she ended her sentence, but a voice spoke her name.

"Mary!"

She didn't dare move but her heart beat madly. Then it came again, stronger. No imaginary voice, this! She sprang up, overturning her chair and dropping her pen so the ink scattered over her gown.

"O'Hara!" she cried.

There he was in the room, thinner, older, the lines on his face deeper, his right arm in a sling. They were transfixed, gazing at each other, all feeling but wonder momentarily paralysed.

It was such a strange and unbelievable experience; so much that couldn't ever be expressed or understood was crammed into that splinter of time. Mary was shaking as though she had the ague and she couldn't run forward and throw her arms round him for she hadn't the power to move.

Her voice trembled when she spoke and her words sounded formal in her ears: "How—how glad I am to see you, O'Hara," she said.

How glad! She meant to say so much but all the ecstatic greetings that should have poured out spontaneously dried up into those few poor words.

But the sound of her voice seemed to release him and he strode towards her, put his left arm round her and kissed her.

"My dear, dear Mary," he said.

To have him there, to know he was safe, to feel the stuff of his coat, to put up her hand and touch his cheek and gradually to become accustomed to the reality of him was all that mattered.

"I've been afraid we might never meet again," she whispered.

"And I at times. I thought of you continually and swore if ever we met I'd say what's been in my heart for years. My dear, dear soul, it is that I love you!"

She was so still, so quiet.

"I love you," he said again.

"O'Hara!"

She sank down on the sofa and drew him down beside her and he gazed at her with such affection and thankfulness as moved her to lean her head on his shoulder and weep.

"You've suffered. I can see you have," she sobbed.

"Only tell me you love me and it will be forgotten."

"I do. Indeed I do. I never knew it till Barnes

came and said you were taken prisoner and he feared the worst for you. Then it burst on me. It was like a million candles lighting up the world and my life has been different ever since."

"What a fool I was not to speak before I went away! But I had so little hope then. In prison I swore I'd tell you if ever I got free even if you laughed me to scorn."

"I've had so much time to think of you and every recollection made you dearer to me," she said. "I think I'd have run mad if it hadn't been for Anne Damer for she has had to bear with all my outpourings—all my fears and hopes and miseries and joys!"

"So the Stick proved a friend indeed," he said. "My dear Mary, I come from Park Place where she told me everything. I begin almost to like her."

"I only wish you would!" she said.

"If you wish it I shall. Your wishes are my commands. She wrote you a letter and here it is. Oh Mary, my dear, I quite loved her when she told me how you'd run through the streets to her the night Barnes came to you. You can't guess the emotions that flooded through me at that. That you, so lovely, with so many friends, should care for me who have nothing to offer you but a heart full of love."

"I always liked you better than anyone else. Always. I shall always like you the best of all, but now I love you, too."

He kissed the hand he held and then her cheek and then he kissed her lips and the beating of her heart almost frightened her.

"You are my dear Irresistible," he said.

The sound of voices in the hall made them draw away from each other and Mr. Berry came in.

"Why, my dear, dear O'Hara!" he exclaimed. "What an unlooked for and wonderful surprise it is to find you here! I scarcely know how to express my delight in seeing you again, or my thankfulness at your safe return. We must drink your health."

He fussed about, pouring the wine, offering congratulations, asking questions and exclaiming over the answers.

"Have you been in Cheltenham long, my dear friend?" he enquired when the first spate of talk subsided.

"I have just arrived," replied O'Hara. "I went to Park Place as soon as I landed and was distressed to see dear Lady Ailesbury so altered by grief. I had hoped I might see my friend, Marshal Conway, again."

"Very sad, very sad," murmured Mr. Berry.

"I suppose Lord Orford is much upset by this? He loved his cousin more than any man on earth," O'Hara said.

"Lord Orford bears up very well," replied Mr. Berry. "He is surprisingly philosophical, as you will notice when you meet. Perhaps I flatter myself, but I think he is able to bear these sorrows so long as my dear girls are there to solace him. Particularly—I can say this as Agnes is out of the way—particularly Mary."

"That's easy enough to understand," said O'Hara, draining his glass to hide the scowl that crossed his face.

"He has been greatly concerned for you—indeed we all were," Mr. Berry went on. "At one time we feared you might share the poor Queen's fate."

"I was lucky not to be shot," O'Hara said. "The French General who held me prisoner got a trouncing for sparing my life but luckily Robespierre fell. Only just in time for men like me."

Mr. Berry tut-tutted and O'Hara launched into an account of his life in the Luxembourg—the card playing, the glee singing, the discomforts, the suspense, the rumours and the awful feeling of terror that pervaded the whole place.

Mary heard their conversation in a sort of trance. She felt herself once removed from the scene, as though she was watching a play. Her father clearly had no idea of the emotions that were stirring so tumultuously in her heart, though as O'Hara related some of the sights he had seen he remarked that she looked pale and wondered if she hadn't better go out of the room.

"Dear Mary has a weak stomach," he explained.

"Mr. Berry's in the right! I'm sure there are more cheerful things to talk of," exclaimed O'Hara. "I came here to recover my health and dwelling on the past is not the way."

"You will dine with us, I hope?" said Mr. Berry. "Your arm doesn't incommode you too much, I trust?"

O'Hara laughed. "I can cut my beef," he said. "I collected this wound at Toulon and it won't heal properly though I was lucky enough to have an

English doctor in my suite. He cared for me devotedly, and I acquired a Negro servant too, who's almost as good to me as poor Rory was.''

Very soon afterwards Agnes came in and expressed the same surprise and pleasure in seeing O'Hara as her father had done.

"How comfortable we shall be now you are here. Everything will be as it used to be, won't it? We've seen little of Cheltenham yet and it's much more pleasant to have a small party for excursions," she said.

"We mustn't tire O'Hara," said Mary.

"Well, of course not! I'm sure he won't allow us to," Agnes replied, and she prattled on about the drives they must take and the people they must visit until Mary escaped with the excuse that she had some orders to give.

O'Hara opened the door for her and when she looked up at him his eyes were full of tenderness but instead of the elation she had always thought she would feel at his return she was bewilderingly sad.

It was as though the tears she had never dared to shed during his absence were waiting to flow, and the moment she gained her own room she was unable to restrain them. She threw herself down on her bed and wept.

She was still there an hour later when Agnes came looking for her.

"Why, dearest Mary, what's the matter?" she asked.

"It's silly and weak of me I know, but I can't help crying," Mary said.

"Why? What's upset you?" Agnes asked.

"It's just that—oh, Agnes—I'm so glad O'Hara's safe home," she sobbed.

Agnes sat down on the bed and patted her sister's shoulder.

"Why, you dear soft-hearted thing, that's no reason to cry," she said. "It would have been different if he'd lost his head. Then you might have wept and I'd have joined you."

"Would you? Would you truly?"

"Indeed I would. Though as he has no wife or family he could have been spared better than some," Agnes said.

Mary sat up straight. "That's the most tragic thing I ever heard!" she exclaimed. "You speak as though no one cares for him."

"We all care for him—but only in the general way of friendship," replied Agnes calmly. "I should be sorry if he came to a bad end, but I wouldn't break my heart."

"I would," Mary said.

"You?" Agnes burst out laughing. "You poor dear, you're suffering from the shock of seeing him so unexpectedly. Or perhaps Cheltenham doesn't agree with you. You'd better have a James powder. That's what Lord Orford would say."

"You don't believe me, do you?" Mary asked.

"Of course I don't," Agnes replied. "But pray do wash your face for you look a fright and you don't want to sit down to dinner all streaked and ugly."

"Dinner!" exclaimed Mary. "I forgot all about it and there are things I must see to."

"Thank heavens we hired the plate with these lodgings," Agnes said. "I hate a poor table."

At that moment Mary was indifferent to the table. She saw that Agnes had no idea of what she felt and wondered how she would take the news of her love for O'Hara and his for her. For the present, she thought, it would be wise to keep it to themselves for she sensed there would be opposition, not only from her own family, but from Lord Orford who was writing every day and seemed determined to prove he couldn't live without her.

16

THERE HAD NEVER been so lovely a September. The harvest was the richest for years and wagons laden with corn filled the roads and held up the coaches. The world took on a hue of gold.

Cheltenham was crowded with visitors and the days were packed with engagements. The Berrys drank the waters, gossiped, walked, shopped, went for drives and attended the twice-weekly balls. O'Hara accompanied them everywhere and Agnes and Mr. Berry said it was just like the old days in Italy.

"But I do think Mary is being noble to give up so many nice things just to sit with him," Agnes remarked one morning when they were at breakfast. "I wouldn't forgo a dance just to sit by his side, I'm afraid."

"Poor fellow! He looks very ill," Mr. Berry said. "Still, I've no doubt a week or so here will make a difference and Mary has a way with invalids."

He buttered a piece of toast and frowned. Then he said: "Agnes takes a sensible view, Mary. A little sacrifice is very well, but not too much, my dear."

Mary marvelled at their blindness. Neither of them had the faintest idea that she and O'Hara were in love. It simply did not occur to them. So she had many opportunities to talk with him and they decided nobody should know of the understanding between them but Mrs. Damer.

She was happy. "When we are married . . . " she thought, and the words acted like a charm opening up new vistas before her. To live with O'Hara, to share the same roof, the same bed, to take all their meals together, to walk, talk, to make love. Perhaps to have children.

He was as happy as she.

"I'm so happy," she said.

"And when we're married I shall be so proud! I shan't fear snubs or be afraid of what people may say about me," she went on. "I shan't know myself when I have you to lean on."

"I think I shall lean on you," he said. "I shall become as dependent as Lord Orford and ten times more demanding."

He said it with a smile, but she shivered and put her hand over his mouth.

"Hush! Don't speak to him. I don't want to think of the obstacles in my way. I shall overcome them, never fear, but let's be happy—let's enjoy the present."

But in the next breath she was talking of the future.

"After so long abroad would it not please you to have a home command?" she asked.

"If it would please *you*, Mary."

"I'm sure you deserve something less onerous and if you have a post at home we'll have a house in London, won't we?"

"If you think we can afford it, my dearest."

"Oh, I'm sure we can. I've worked it all out. You told me the limit we might go to and we shall live comfortably. We'll be able to rent a pleasant house, keep our carriage and horses with three men servants and four women and allow about ten pounds a week for housekeeping."

"You astound me! How on earth do you know all this?"

"Through keeping house for Pa. Of course, coal is an item. It'll cost us fifty pounds a year and we shall have to allow another hundred and twenty-five for wine and beer. Oh, and another twenty-five for candles."

"Candles! You think of everything," he said.

"I shall revel in my housekeeping and in entertaining. We'll give choice little dinner parties and invite all our favourites. Can't you see us receiving them?"

"I rather think I can," he said. "You'll be the prettiest, smartest and most fascinating little hostess in town and I shall be the most envied of men."

"And when they've gone—that'll be the best time, won't it? When we sit by the fire and watch the ashes gather and stir a log to see the sparks fly up. And then when we take our candles from the hall table and go upstairs—oh, I shan't care how the wind howls outside then. I shan't care how fierce the world is with you at my side."

He took her hand and measured it against his. It looked small and white against his darker skin.

"Can it be true that you love me?" he asked. "Am I to believe it?"

"Do you doubt it?"

"Sometimes."

"But why?"

"I only have to think of what I am to be full of misgivings. So much older, so battered, with neither riches nor family . . . "

"If you speak like that I shall be angry," she said. "Don't ever doubt our happiness away."

"Then never leave me," he said.

"Never."

The golden days continued, but the leaves began to flutter down. The Virginia creepers were a vivid crimson and the sun slanted through the trees. She dreaded the idea of returning to Twickenham and of entering the bewitched domain of Strawberry Hill.

If, when they married, they could live in England for a time all could be managed, she thought. Her family would accept the situation and Lord Orford would become reconciled to it. But thinking of them depressed her and thinking of O'Hara was exhilarating. She thought only of him, of his endearments, his caresses.

A letter from Anne Damer arrived and after reading it hastily she almost bubbled over with excitement. They were to leave Cheltenham next day but one and she and O'Hara both realized they would not have the same freedom once she was back at Cliveden, but Mrs. Damer's letter sent her soaring to the skies.

"Anne has invited me to Park Place in October and you are to be there too," she told him at the first opportunity. "She's writing to you separately, but she tells me Lady Ailesbury will be away so we shall be all to ourselves. Only think of it!"

"God above! I can scarcely wait!" he said. "I should know what my future is to be by then and we shall be able to make our plans in peace."

"What a good friend Anne is!" exclaimed Mary warmly. "Who else would be so thoughtful for us? Don't you love her for her kindness?"

"If you tell me to I suppose I must," he replied.

"She will do anything, no matter what it costs her, for our happiness," Mary said. "She writes with such sincerity and is so staunch and true to me and I know she longs for your approbation. She'll break her heart if you dislike her once we are married."

"I see I must sink my prejudices. For your sake I'd do more, and I certainly bless the Stick for her kind invitation. Tell her so when you answer."

"I'll write straight away," said Mary delightedly.

O'Hara left for London the next evening. He was much better in health, had gained weight and his colour had returned. When he took leave of her Mary longed to proclaim that this magnificent man was her promised husband and that she was soon to be Mrs. Charles O'Hara.

They watched him ride away and she was so full of love and pride that tears started in her eyes and Agnes saw them.

"Heavens! You're never crying because O'Hara's gone, are you?" she exclaimed.

"I'm in love with him," said Mary, unable to contain herself any longer.

"With O'Hara? Nonsense! How could you be? You'd have to kiss that blue-black chin of his!"

"And so I have done, many times, and shall do many more, I hope," said Mary, gaining courage as she made her confession.

"Pa, did you hear that?" Agnes exclaimed, running after Mr. Berry who had returned to the house. "Mary says she's in love with O'Hara!"

She sounded so incredulous that Mary wanted to shake her, and her father was no less so. His mouth dropped open and he goggled at her for an eternity before he spoke.

"My dear child, can you be serious?" he asked eventually. "Does he love you?"

"He says he does," replied Mary, "and I was never more serious in my life. I always liked him, Pa. Better than anyone. When he was taken prisoner I knew it was a lot more than mere liking and when we met here we simply fell in love."

"Does he speak of marriage?" Mr. Berry asked. "Dear me, this is most disconcerting. So totally unlooked for! I never would have suspected it.

Why, he must be nearly as old as I am!"

Suddenly Agnes uttered a loud wail and sank down on the floor.

"What are we to do without Mary?" she cried. "How are you and I to manage, Pa? She's not thinking of us at all—she's just thinking of herself and proposing to run off and desert us, and with a friend of the family, too! A fine friend he is, to sneak in and steal her when we never suspected anything!"

"Hush, Agnes. You jangle my nerves!" said Mr. Berry, putting his fingers in his ears.

"I shall be left all alone! An old maid with a pittance to live on! I shall end my days in an almshouse going out picking up firewood!" wailed Agnes, louder still. "This is the end of everything!"

"But you would marry if you wanted to," expostulated Mary. "Why shouldn't I?"

"Because you are the elder and have always looked after us," returned Agnes. "It would be a very different thing for me. You've always said you wanted me to marry."

"And I meant it," Mary said.

"But I never said I wanted you to. We're not a marrying family. Look at poor darling Pa. He could have married scores of times over but he never did because he was so fond of us. He's devoted his life to us. And besides all that, what on earth can you see in O'Hara as a husband?"

"All I want to see," Mary said.

"But he's always on active service and he's always in debt and he's got no family either. And besides, he's a terrible man of the town and no wonder with a father like Lord Tyrawley!''

''Agnes!'' quavered Mr. Berry weakly.

''And when he's not gallivanting round the town he's in a ship going off to some dreadful battle or else he's languishing in prison waiting to have his head chopped off!'' pursued Agnes.

''That is enough!'' cried Mr. Berry. ''I can't bear to hear another word. You have a voice like a corncrake, Agnes. I shall go to bed and I advise you both to do the same. We will talk of this further in the morning.''

Mary spent a miserable night. She had always been afraid her father would not face the prospect of her contemplated marriage and would behave as though it was never going to take place, but she had hoped for a little kindness from Agnes.

''Not a single word of congratulation or good wishes,'' she thought. ''Thank heavens O'Hara wasn't present.''

She could not have borne to see her family's weaknesses exposed even to him. Already she was making excuses for them. Poor Agnes wasn't really selfish, only frightened at the thought of being left with her father unsupported. She knew their dispositions so well and loved them so devotedly that she understood their feelings although they had both hurt her terribly.

Next morning Agnes said she felt far too shaken to get up and Mary was miserable when she saw her sister's tear-streaked face.

Mr. Berry came into the breakfast room looking more pensive than usual and he stirred his tea ponderously for a long time. Then he told her he had slept very ill and hoped she had fared better.

"Your news of last night shook me so much that if I didn't know you so well I should have thought you were joking," he said.

"I thought you liked O'Hara," she pleaded.

"And so I do, my dear. Why, we must have known him ten years by now and I look on him as one of ourselves. But there are a great many things to consider. One of them is his mode of life which has always been so unsettled. I hoped you would marry a man of substance and family. You are accustomed to a modest degree of comfort now."

"But comfort isn't everything, Pa dear," Mary argued. "I love O'Hara with all my heart and would willingly forgo comfort for his sake. Heaven knows he bore enough for us as a prisoner."

"That was the fortune of war which he would be the first to admit," Mr. Berry reminded her. "But I must confess I'm surprised and disappointed to observe that other considerations don't seem to have entered your head."

"What considerations, Pa?" asked Mary.

"Financial ones. You always keep a close eye on our affairs so doesn't it occur to you that we shall be a great deal worse off by your leaving us?"

"Better off, I should think, Pa. You won't have the expense of my victuals and wearing apparel."

"Do you suppose that I, your own father, could let you go to your husband a pauper? Without a mite to call your own?" he expostulated.

"Pa dear, O'Hara won't care. He knows we've nothing so he won't expect anything," she said patiently.

"We have our pride, thank God."

Mr. Berry took a loud gulp of tea, crunched some toast and then went on: "We have our pride, Mary. Consequently I shall give you the small portion to which you are entitled. Miserable as it is it is what you would inherit at my death. As you know only too well the annuity from my brother ceases when I die, but the capital sum from Uncle Ferguson remains and you shall have your share of it on marriage."

"But there's no necessity for that," Mary reiterated. "Oh God, I never thought that when I wished to marry we would talk of nothing but money and capital and income. I thought my happiness might at least be mentioned. I thought I might be congratulated on having won the love of a man like O'Hara."

"You know as well as I that money contributes to happiness and that without it life is sheer misery. Have you forgotten your childhood?"

"Indeed I have not, but pray don't make me miserable now by alluding to it. Oh Pa, I little thought that you would dash my spirits like this! I thought you would be gratified by my alliance with a man as noble and valiant as my O'Hara."

"My dear Mary, my only wish is for your happiness and if you can bring yourself to break up our little family circle and enjoy yourself outside it you will never hear me complain."

With that Mr. Berry opened his newspaper and Mary saw it would be useless for her to say any more. He soon recovered his good spirits, and by the time they were ready to leave for home the next day it was almost as though nothing had happened.

He had simply shelved the idea—and so had Agnes. O'Hara was not mentioned any more.

17

LORD ORFORD WAS having a new ice-house built and the Berrys were to share all its advantages. They were sleeping at Strawberry Hill on their first night home from Cheltenham in case, as he feared, Cliveden might not be properly aired and, although Mrs. Richardson indignantly assured them that it was, they gave in to him.

He had been thinking how pleased they would be with the ice-house all the time he had been planning it and now they were with him he was gay and jubilant in spite of the pain from his gout.

"I was *unked* without you, my dearest dears," he said fondly. "But what of that? Now you will both be well throughout the winter so my deprivation these past few weeks will bring me future comfort. And now what of O'Hara? I envied him being with you at Cheltenham. Still, he deserved some delight after all he suffered in France, poor fellow!''

Neither Mr. Berry nor Agnes seemed inclined to satisfy Lord Orford's curiosity so Mary was forced to speak for all of them and give an account of their excursions and frivolities.

Feeling the bright old eyes on her, her heart began to palpitate most uncomfortably, but Lord Orford gave no sign of suspecting anything, and when he had all her news he went into a long account of all their Twickenham friends and had a wealth of kind messages from them for his dear Berrys which he proceeded to deliver with sundry well-aimed side swipes at the senders.

As usual the whole family were convulsed by his remarks and their amusement encouraged him, but although Mary laughed as much as any of them she saw how careful she would have to be to escape from the snares of Lord Orford without destroying the delicate fabric of their friendship. She counted his affection for them all as their greatest gift from fortune. A break would be unthinkable, but how could he be induced to relax his possessiveness? The problem was with her constantly.

The weather still held when she set off for Park Place a few days later and once she was clear of Twickenham and settled back in the carriage she revelled in thoughts of the few days ahead.

Perhaps O'Hara would have news of his posting and if he had they could make plans. She tried not to think of the upheaval her marriage would cause—she wanted to be free of anxiety for this little time.

They made good speed on the road and when she arrived she was told Mrs. Damer and the General were in the garden. The late afternoon sun still shone.

"Don't announce me—I'll go out to them," she told the servant.

Mrs Damer and O'Hara were sitting under the thorn tree so deep in conversation that she wanted to steal up and take them by surprise but they had heard voices and looked up. O'Hara leapt to his feet, came to meet her and greeted her as exuberantly as a boy, drawing her arm through his. He no longer wore a sling and she thought she had never seen him look so well and so handsome and so—she would once have laughed at the thought—thrilling.

"How well O'Hara looks!" she exclaimed, as she greeted Mrs. Damer. "You and Park Place have done wonders for him."

"I incline to think that you have restored him, Mary," Anne Damer said.

"And what were you talking of as I crossed the lawn? You had your heads so close together you must have been hatching a plot!"

"Of you! O'Hara has no other subject. How could he have?"

"Then I'll leave you to continue," Mary laughed. "I trust you to remember every flattering thing he says and repeat it to me afterwards," and she ran off into the laurel walk but O'Hara came after her and clasped her in his arms. Suddenly all the joy and ecstasy she had never known in youth flooded through her. Her whole being was transformed.

"I adore you. When shall we be married?"

"When?" Her voice was a little breathless echo of his. "I haven't thought of when."

"Then think now. You mean to marry me, I hope?"

"Indeed, I think I shall die if I don't."

But she couldn't think because she had lost her head and only had a heart.

"Then name a day. Any day of the week, only let it be within the next month."

"So soon? You're smiling, O'Hara! I believe you're keeping something from me. Has your command come through?"

He nodded. He was so pleased he could hardly keep the smile from his face.

"I am appointed Governor of Gibraltar at last," he said.

It came like a spear of ice. "Gibraltar?"

"I've wanted this for a long, long time."

"Yes," she said. "You should have had it years ago."

"Aren't you going to congratulate me?"

But she felt a terrible oppression, just as though she was being crushed in a cage. There were the heavy, vivid burning, dying colours of the autumn all round her, flaming leaves moved in a still-warm breeze and she was there confronting him and he had doubt and disbelief in his eyes.

"You are not pleased," he said.

Cold. She had never seen him cold before.

So many thoughts crowded her mind that she couldn't express one of them. She could hear a chorus of discordant voices: her father's plaintive tones, Agnes's half-hysterical outbursts, and Lord Orford's querulous and reproachful.

"I see you don't care. I have been mistaken in you," he said.

But her love for him was all-pervasive. It surrounded her; it was the centre of her life, the very heart of it. If she could but make him believe it!

There was a note of pleading now when he spoke. "My dear, dear soul, I know it would please you if I could be stationed nearer home but now, at last, my chance has come. And with you beside me . . . "

She didn't care where they went—anywhere under the sky so long as they could be together. Her concern was for the others but she could not bring herself to say so, to harp on the cares that beset her. She felt like a fly in a spider's web, the silken bonds binding closer and closer round her, every limb fettered while her mind and heart stayed free and almost burst with longing.

She gazed up at him towering over her and she begged for help and strength, not in words, but in an intensity of feeling.

He placed his hands on her shoulders. "Will you come with me, Mary? Will you be my wife?" he asked.

He was asking her to disrupt the lives of all those who depended upon her, those for whom she had so painfully and selflessly cared. She could not accept. She must have been mad ever to have thought she could. Reasons, reasons, reasons. They poured in and they were all against her fervent, burning wish. Would she go with him, would she be his wife? The answer was an unequivocal no.

But . . .

"Yes!"

Her voice lifted clear and strong. "I love you with all my heart and soul, O'Hara. I want to be your wife more than anything in the world."

Those days at Park Place were the happiest she had ever known. She felt, without any concrete reason, that all her difficulties would be smoothed out and as she walked in the gardens with O'Hara she was amazed to find how well he understood them. They strolled through green arcades and stopped by the fountain to hold their joined hands in the cascading water and he told her to calm her fears. He knew the claims her family had on her. He talked in the comfortable way she loved, making everything seem easy.

They went into the library where Mrs. Damer sat and he continued with his ideas.

"When we are married you will be as much theirs as ever you were," he declared. "Your father and Agnes can join us in Gibraltar and you may tell them from me we keep excellent company on the Rock."

Mary was comforted by this but O'Hara saw that Anne Damer was watching her with hungry eyes. In his own excess of happiness he felt a sudden tenderness for her.

"And the dear Stick, too," he said. "She shall be with us as much as she wants. Hang it all, when happiness overflows doesn't it engulf us all?"

Mrs. Damer put down the book she had been pretending to read.

"He is indeed a wonderful being, Mary!" she exclaimed and she took his hand and said in a desperate rush: "She is my other self, O'Hara. My far better self. God knows how I suffer in all that affects her—all I pray for is her happiness and yours. When she leaves England with you my heart will go with you both. Perhaps, some day when fate permits, I may join you on your Rock. Till then . . ."

Her words were lost in a sob and she hurried from the room. O'Hara stared after her.

"God knows how a pair like Conway and Lady Ailesbury could have brought forth so odd a daughter!" he said. "Why can't she sizzle with passion for a man?"

"You could go a long way and never find a truer friend," said Mary.

"Far too dangerous a friend for my wife," he replied. "She'll be jealous of the happiness you find in marriage. She had none herself, poor wretch. That's why she footles about with bits of marble and crazy ideas about liberty and equality for women. I don't care to think of her instilling her revolutionary ideas into your nimble brain."

"My nimble brain is entirely occupied by thoughts of you so you need have no fear of anyone else crowding you out," she said. "Dear, beloved O'Hara, let us talk only of ourselves for I've no room for others in this interlude we've stolen."

He took her face between his hands and kissed her. "We haven't stolen it. This is our life," he said. "All the rest is the interlude."

18

MARY WAS CONVINCED O'Hara misjudged Anne Damer and he was soon forced to agree with her for Anne told Mary plainly that it was her duty to inform Lord Orford of her intention to marry without loss of time.

"He will be angry at first," she said. "But when he reflects he'll realise he can't expect you to sacrifice the best of your life for him. Just think, Mary. He's nearly eighty. And he won't be deserted, I promise you. I shall be with him as much as my mother can spare me, and Agnes won't neglect him."

"The mere thought of telling him turns my blood to water," Mary said. "I'm not indispensable, who is? But what shall I say? How begin? I shall shake to pieces."

"You wouldn't tremble if you had a different bridegroom to present," remarked O'Hara. "He'd swell with pride if you married a duke and give you away himself. But to marry me! I bow my head in shame at the thought of my parentage."

"O come! I've often heard Lord Orford laugh to split his sides over Lord Tyrawley's cracks," Mrs. Damer said.

"And in the next breath he proclaims him the most licentious man of his day," O'Hara said. "And I've no fortune and am generally solvent for no more than four days a year. Mary, my dear, when I think of what I am I wish I were a better man. This is a most imprudent marriage."

"A fig for prudence!" she exclaimed. "I hate it. I don't know anyone who could hold a candle to you, and who cares for titles and show?"

"Lord Orford does," replied O'Hara, but he was glowing in the warmth of her admiration. "He'll give you a thousand reasons why you shouldn't have me."

"I shall refute them all. I shall have arguments, too."

"Bravo!"

"If he had an inkling it would be easier."

"He has," said Mrs. Damer darkly. "None so blind, my dears."

But they weren't dashed, even by this. They returned to Cliveden full of confidence and before leaving for town O'Hara set all his hopes and plans before Mr. Berry who listened as though they conveyed little to him or were to be realised in a future so distant as to be virtually out of sight.

Mary tried to look cheerful when she saw him off but she could feel an atmosphere hanging over Cliveden and when she returned to her father he did not meet her eyes.

"Lord Orford has been fretting wretchedly for you," he said. "He is not at all well. Pray go to him at once. And, Mary, say nothing to him of O'Hara."

"But Pa, don't you think I should pave the way?"

"Not now. It would do irreparable harm."

"But how long can I delay?"

Mr. Berry shook his head ponderously. "Patience," he said.

She hurried out and across the garden which was dark except for the light from their windows. A night owl hooted and she drew her shawl round her shoulders for the air was chill from the river and a mist was rising.

They told her Lord Orford was in the library. She ran up the stairs where the great painted lantern threw its rich colours down, hurried past the cold suits of armour and the gleaming weapons that adorned the Armoury and went into the library where Lord Orford sat huddled in a chair with his eyes closed. He looked almost lifeless, so frail and thin and pallid. She noticed his watch was on the table beside him.

"Lord Orford," she whispered.

He was awake in an instant. "Oh, my dear lamb, I thought you'd forgotten me," he said. "I've been so anxious thinking you might be ill. But I expect you were kept by more congenial company."

"No, I assure you. We were talking at home and the time slipped by," she said.

"Too fast, too fast!" His voice grew querulous. "Holy Virgin, I shan't live to bother you long! Just a few more months—perhaps only weeks. You weary of me."

"Oh no! How can you think such a thing?"

She was overcome by pity for him: so old, lonely and in so much pain.

"If I could but count on seeing you every day—if only for a few minutes—the trials my wretched infirmities thrust on me would be easy to bear. You have time for others—for Mrs. Damer and a host of other people, but you grudge it to me."

"That's not true, and it's unkind," she said.

"You haven't been near me for months!" he accused. "I've waited and waited in vain. You forgot me."

"But try to recollect. I was with you only the night before I went to Park Place. Don't you recollect we read some of Mr. Gray's poems and you spoke so kindly of him and told me of your travels together? Don't you remember that?"

"Was that so short a time ago?" he asked uneasily.

"Yes. And we were to read some more tonight. Shall I fetch the book?"

"Why, my dear sweet Mary, is this really true? Yes, of course it is! I remember now. You wore your blue silk and looked enchanting. Of course I remember. How did I come to forget?"

He rang for more candles, he could not have

enough candles, and when they were brought in and Mary fetched the book of poems and sat down to read the soft light fell on her hair.

Lord Orford leaned back and his eyes roved round his library with its ornately carved cases, its glowing colours, its vibrant reds and blues—ceiling, windows, bookbindings—they were all alive with colour. But none of his treasures mattered to him now unless Mary was there. She was his breath of life.

As the days and evenings passed Lord Orford's dependence on her seemed to increase and although she knew that no word of her engagement had reached him it was almost as though he sensed an imminent change and was striving by all the means in his power to bind her to him.

In spite of Mr. Berry's warning she often tried to bring the conversation round to marriage but each time she had a sentence formulated Lord Orford cut in with a subject that took them off on an entirely different track and gave her no opportunity to get back. It was as thought they were playing a game of chance in which he always held the winning hand for he seemed to know she had something to tell him and he fenced with a mental dexterity that completely defeated her.

And all the time she was thinking about her new life, she took refuge in her thoughts of it at every chance. She wanted new clothes for Gibraltar and had asked Sally to make them. She chose silks, satins and delicate muslins and once O'Hara went with her. Oh, the joy of fingering that magnificent rich brocade!

"It's a terrible extravagance," she said.

"But there's nothing too fine for the Governor's lady!"

She would be standing by his side in it; they would be at the top of a fine marble staircase with a wrought-iron balustrade and the company would come rustling up, and she, Mary Berry, would be there to receive them with the man she would love till her dying day.

Sally soon realised why she wanted so many dresses and in a burst of confidence Mary let her into the secret. It was bliss to talk to her and to see her wide-eyed delight. There wasn't anyone else she could consult about clothes; Anne Damer had lost all interest in them and slouched about in her father's old coat; Agnes was wrapped up so tightly in her own woes she might have been a chrysalis in a cocoon but Sally liked nothing better than fashion and when she heard Mary's plans she was as pleased as though half the joy was hers.

She could be trusted not to talk but when they were together she could never contain herself and went into raptures over the General, recounting his goodness to Mary and his kindness to her when he came back from France.

"He came to see me, Miss Mary. He did, indeed, even though he'd suffered so in that prison he still came to comfort me and to talk of my Rory. He sat there, on the very chair you're sitting on now, and he took my Molly on his knee and he made us so proud."

Mary felt proud herself as Sally spoke. It was just like O'Hara to think of Sally and her children.

"You'll make a wonderful pair, Miss Mary, my dear. I never saw a finer looking man or a kinder one and I can't think of a better husband for you or a better wife for him. Lawks, he may be a bit gay, but so was my Rory and none the worse for it!"

"I couldn't abide a saintly husband!" Mary said.

"No more could I! I always preferred spice to sugar. But I'm glad you're to be so well settled. To tell the truth I thought you might be going to marry the old gentleman when there was all that talk!"

"Heavens no! There was never any fear of that. I'm far too fond of my dear old friend to do him the injustice of marrying him. And besides, Sally, he never asked me. You may repeat that to any of your inquisitive ladies if they pry and you'll be speaking the truth. He never asked me."

She walked on air whenever she was away from Strawberry Hill; it was a new and exhilarating life she was living full of hope and promise, but she kept her balance and spent her evenings with Lord Orford and was more thoughtful than she had ever been. She had so much happiness to spare.

But in the mornings she would have her horse saddled and canter across the meadows to meet O'Hara. Neither her father nor Agnes ever asked where she was going; they didn't refer to her engagement or behave as though there was to be any change in her life.

"I'm not in the least surprised your father is so absent," Mrs. Damer remarked. "But Agnes! What possesses her to be so obtuse? And so gloomy? She is being thoroughly selfish and you must ignore it. She'll get over it and be pleased about your marriage."

"I'm sure they will both accept the change situation in time, but what of Lord Orford, Anne? He persists that I neglect him, and I don't. Sometimes he's so cross and peevish I could weep!"

"It's just like him to be so. He suspects, and you must be firm with him. The more you give the more he will demand, my dear. I've known him since I was a tot. He'll come round."

"I wish I could think so."

"Believe so. He's got his wits still, all his teeth and his eyes and his ears and he sleeps like a dormouse, so why does he complain? You mustn't waste any more of your youth."

"It's almost gone," Mary said.

"Then garner it. I was with him when he had his dinner yesterday, and what a revolting dinner it was—to say nothing of the way he ate it. He shared it with that mangy cat of his and they might have been taken for twins. I wonder they didn't both vomit on the same plate for dessert!"

Mrs. Damer was bridling with indignation, and she looked so angry with her hands thrust deep in the pockets of the man's coat she wore and her big, clumsy boots.

"Marry the man," she said. "Go off to Gibraltar and hang everyone, me included!"

And that was what Mary wanted to do, though not so drastically, but from the way her family behaved she would have thought O'Hara a figment of her imagination if she hadn't met him daily. But the moment they met and she felt his strong hand on hers he was the reality, her other life the dream.

They would gallop through the Petersham fields where the mists hung blue in the trees and the exhilaration of the tangy air with its sting of approaching winter brought colour to her face. She thought and spoke of their future continually.

One day O'Hara told her he would soon know the date of his departure and he warned her to speak to Lord Orford immediately. This brought a check to her high spirits. She slowed her mount to a walking pace.

"How I wish I'd never consented to live at Cliveden. You were right when you told me I'd regret it," she said.

"I hope I'll be proved wrong, Mary."

"It went against all my instincts."

"You owe Lord Orford a debt of gratitude which you've discharged a thousand times over," he said. "You are very fond of him and he of you. Affection doesn't exact payment. Think of this when you feel apprehensive. And, you know, the dear Stick is quite sure he'll only be temporarily upset and she knows him better than any of us."

"I hope she's right. She sustains me at every turn and cheers me on, but he isn't so fretful with her, or so demanding."

"She's not you, my dear. But she does her best. Now don't start to berate me—I try to appreciate her, damnable boots and all. Listen, my sweetest. My orders may come today. Speak to him now."

"Oh, my God!"

"If you love me you will."

"Then today it shall be," she said after a pause.

There was one of those strange moments when the whole of a lifetime seems to pass and it is impossible to tell afterwards if it is still the same hour, the same day, the same week.

During this extraordinary lapse momentous changes took place and Mary felt as though she was gaining a new consciousness and her timidity, her doubts, fears, fell away like a ragged old cloak. In their stead came courage and a sudden uplifting valour. She was ready to face dragons.

She couldn't wait to do battle.

"Race me!" she challenged, and she spurred her horse and sped across the meadows towards Strawberry Hill leaving O'Hara far behind.

19

IF HER HORSE would only run faster! She was miles ahead in spirit, already at Strawberry and pouring out her news to Lord Orford—not in fear and trembling—but with exultation.

"Dear Lord Orford, I've something wonderful to tell you! I am in love and have been asked in marriage. You'll be happy for me, won't you—and give us your blessing?"

She wouldn't give him time to think. She would race on about O'Hara: "You like him and hold him in such high esteem. Why, whenever you two meet you talk to me! You've often teased me about it—and then you were so sorry because I was cast down when he didn't get the promotion he deserved. But now—oh, Lord Orford, my dearest, most sincerely loved friend, I want to share my joy with you more than with anyone else!"

The portraits in the Great Parlour would look down: his father, his mother, his friends, all pictured as he loved them and if he wished for a picture of her surely he would want it to reveal her joy in the possession of O'Hara with the fulfilment that marrying him would bring.

They would have children to bring to Strawberry. He had loved them when he was younger, had petted and adored Anne Damer as a child, and once he grew accustomed to the idea would he not like to see her children racing and romping in his beloved riverside meadows?

Even if he refused to admit it to begin with wouldn't the idea of life going on refuse to be suppressed and eventually win? She felt certain of it as she threw the reins to William outside the stables at Cliveden.

"Wonderful morning, ma'am!"

"Heavenly, William." She ran indoors to change.

As she reached the staircase her father came out of his study. Her hand was on the banister, her hair hung in loose curls and her face was glowing. She smiled at him.

"I wish to speak with you, Mary," he said in an agitated tone.

"Now, Pa? Won't it do later?"

"I had hoped to see you before you went out," he answered.

She followed him into the study, he closed the door and began to pace up and down and clear his throat nervously.

"You look quite ominous, Pa. What on earth's the matter? Has Washington asked you to raise his wages again?" she asked.

"I shall come straight to the point. I had an interview with Lord Orford after you left him last night," Mr. Berry began. "What passed must never be repeated, but I know I can depend on your discretion. However, will you promise never to divulge what I am about to tell you?"

"If you want me to. I promise. There! But whatever was it? Did you tell him about O'Hara and me?"

"O'Hara wasn't mentioned," replied Mr. Berry. "The fact is that Lord Orford wishes to appoint me as his literary executor and I have accepted the office gladly, but of course it is quite understood between us that the work will devolve on you. He merely puts in my name to save you the embarrassment of using yours."

"As Mrs. Charles O'Hara I should not be in the least embarrassed," Mary said. "I should be proud."

"Any plans you may have for marrying O'Hara must be deferred indefinitely, my dear."

"But Pa, we are to be married very soon!"

"With Lord Orford so plagued by the rheumatism and gout that he has had to take to his bed? He can neither write nor hold a book! He is very, very peevish and put out."

"Yes, Pa. I know he is. But he'll recover. He always does."

"He will not recover if you desert him. Mary, you force me to tell you more than I intended. God knows I wished to spare you this. I hoped your sense of duty as a daughter and as a sister would have inspired you to postpone this marriage.''

"To postpone it? Heaven knows O'Hara has waited long enough! He'll run out of patience altogether. But what can you have to tell me?''

"Simply that Lord Orford has told me the terms of his will as it affects us. I need hardly say that this must not be mentioned outside these four walls.''

"Well?''

"This house, Cliveden, is left outright to you and Agnes together with a sum of money to enable you to live at our present level when I am gone.''

He waited. She was too stunned to answer but she felt trapped. It was just as though she was in a room and the door slammed shut and became invisible, merging in with the walls so that there was no sign of an exit.

"I beg you to think carefully of what I am telling you,'' her father went on. "Reflect on our misfortunes, Mary. You know well what our position was when you were a child. You remember the anxiety, the deprivations, the grinding care?''

"But that's all past . . .''

"If anything happens to make Lord Orford change his will I dread to think what would become to poor Agnes. She would be almost destitute.''

"Lord Orford would never spite her so, even if he cut me out and upon my soul I wish he would!''

"You are not thinking, Mary. You are deep in debt to Lord Orford for all the attention he has shown you and Agnes. Are you going to desert him in his hour of need?''

"God! I wish we'd never taken this house. I knew it would cause misery and mortification. What a fool I was to be persuaded! A fine thing my principles are when my conduct puts me in bondage!"

"I don't understand you, my dear."

"Pa, I am in love. I love O'Hara. You say Lord Orford needs me, but before heaven, O'Hara needs me, too. Are you asking me to choose between them?"

"It is not a question of choice—simply one of patience," said Mr. Berry in an injured tone.

"I've no patience left. I am going to tell Lord Orford everything and await the outcome," she retorted and she went to the door knowing that once outside she would be free.

But as she touched the handles she heard a sob and looking back saw her father was in tears. She felt a horrifying, almost degrading sense of pity. She hesitated for he had slid from his chair to his knees and was clutching at his desk and babbling incoherently of his wasted life, his terrible failure, his overwhelming misery. It all came gushing out in a jumbled account which she knew far too well but had never heard recounted with such bitterness.

He led her through it all—he showed her her mother, snatched so early from him and she saw, for the first time, his insurmountable grief and the way it had wrecked him.

She had always revered him for his devotion to her mother but she never realised till then how his loss had crippled him, robbing him of energy and initiative and rendering him incapable of making decisions and rebuilding his life.

He had been firm in one thing only—his refusal to remarry and provide the son who would have secured his fortune.

"But I couldn't put any other woman in your mother's place, Mary," he said. "Not for a fortune—not for any consideration in the world!"

He had done everything else he could to regain his place in his uncle's esteem and had failed. But then had come the soft years, the interlude of success, of establishing a place for themselves, of being singled out by Lord Orford. And it was all her doing. He knew well enough that he and Agnes owed everything to her good sense, her gift for gaining and keeping friends.

"But this will all go," he said. "Lord Orford will turn us out and we shall be ostracised by everyone. Think of your poor sister! How is she to face the world without you to guide her?"

"What reason have you to think Lord Orford would be so cruel?" she asked. All her colour had gone now.

"He is ill and in pain. He accuses you of neglecting him and is bitter and reproachful. If he knew your plans he could retaliate in a way to hurt us."

"You are unjust to him."

"The risk is too grave to take," her father said.

"So you are asking me to renounce the man I love so you and Agnes may keep your comforts and your place in society? But O'Hara has promised his house will be open to you. Your home would be with us. And if you should die, which heaven send won't be for years, do you think O'Hara and I would have no room for Agnes?''

"Must you remind me of my failure?'' pleaded Mr. Berry, with tears streaming down his face. "Do you think I don't feel my inability to leave poor Agnes provided for? O'Hara has no fortune, and if he had do you think she would stoop to take it? I believed you loved your sister well enough to have no doubt of the course you should take.''

She couldn't bear her father's wretchedness and the way his eyes never left her as he pleaded. Oh, if she had only gone and slammed the door and left him to his snivelling! If her inborn, protective sense had only deserted her!

At last she said: "So you want me to send O'Hara away. It will break my heart.''

"My dearest child, I want you to be happy. All I ask is that you persuade him to wait a little longer.''

"Until Lord Orford dies?'' she asked bitterly.

"Heaven forbid! Simply until he's in a more amiable mood. The winter doesn't suit him. We shall all be moving up to town soon and a winter without you would destroy him. Wait, my dear Mary. Later on, with tact and persuasion, you will gradually lead him to accept a parting from you more calmly. But to spring it on him now, so suddenly, would be fatal. Remember, there was no thought of all this two months ago.''

"He may accept, as you say, but how am I to bring O'Hara to do so? He's passionate and hot-blooded. How long must he wait—if he waits?''

"He says he loves you. His patience will prove

it. It need be no longer than it takes an old man to accept a new outlook.''

''If you knew what you are asking! Do you know it, Father?''

''Yes, I do know it,'' he replied.

''And you still ask?''

''I still ask.''

''Then I shall tell O'Hara everything and pray he'll think I have a valid reason for postponement,'' she said.

''He must never know the reason!'' exclaimed Mr. Berry in alarm. ''It must never be spoken of again, even between ourselves. It would be a grave breach of Lord Orford's confidence—and of mine.''

''Then what am I to say?''

''Simply that you can't yet arrange to go. You'll think of a way to embroider the theme.''

''I prefer the truth.''

''It must not be told. I forbid it—and remember, you gave your solemn promise not to repeat a word of this.''

''Oh God, what an unfair way to get a promise!''

''But you'll keep it—for all our sakes?''

''It's too great a burden,'' she said, and she felt it so heavy on her that her shoulders bowed under the weight.

''My dear girl, this is painful for us both—for me in having to admit my inadequacy and see the situation it has brought about; for you in having to part for a little while from your O'Hara. But your disappointment is temporary—mine is with me for life. Your engagement still stands and your marriage will take place a little later than you thought.''

Mary said nothing. She was scarcely capable of thought and her feelings were numb.

''And only think, my dear, you will have the satisfaction of having secured the family's fortunes—a thing I was never able to do.''

She stumbled out of the room and upstairs, gripped in such a vice of misery that she could scarcely drag herself to her bed and once there she buried her head in her pillow and cried for O'Hara with a passion that almost drained her life away.

20

EARLY NEXT MORNING a message arrived from O'Hara asking her to come to Mrs. Damer's in Grosvenor Square. His orders for going had come through at last.

She had slept badly and felt battle-weary and yet with a new day one hope revived and she clung to it tenaciously. She could see that her sudden departure from England would cause utter disruption at Strawberry Hill but, given time, the difficulties might well be smoothed away. Time—that was the vital factor. If O'Hara would only grant her that, if he would only wait, then all would be well.

"I would wait for him through all eternity," she thought, but as she drove through Richmond she saw the place where they had met the previous day and remembered how her heart had lifted at the sight of him. She often passed that way and now she would always feel that catch at the heart, the upward surge of hope that he would be there when there was no possibility that he could be.

The drive to Grosvenor Square was one of the slowest she had ever known for there were associations all the way and by the time she arrived she had lived through lifetimes. And she had to think what to say, and above all what not to say. That was the hardest part—to be obliged to place a guard on her tongue.

At Grosvenor Square she found O'Hara striding up and down the drawing room to the peril of Mrs. Damer's innumerable ornaments and to some of her marble busts which he always said looked exactly alike.

She saw he was in an exuberant mood. He hugged and kissed her and blessed her for coming so soon. "As I knew you would, my dearest Mary. I expect you have charmed the whole of Strawberry Hill into tranquillity and have them all as docile as doves. Did I ever tell you you are a most extraordinary creature?"

She couldn't reply for he kissed her so hard and so long he took her breath away and she didn't know how she would begin to tell him.

"We shan't be disturbed," he said. "The Stick's taken herself off for the day. She's being so considerate I almost love her and I've another of her missives to give you. She does nothing but write to you! She must be half drowned in ink."

Mary took Mrs. Damer's letter and put it away.

She knew what an outpouring it would be—full of praise of O'Hara and encouragement for her with plans and suggestions of how she should go on to further her marriage plans.

"How did Lord Orford take our news?" O'Hara asked. "Badly, I fear, or you'd have been spilling over with joy when you arrived. I thought of you all day yesterday and skulked about Twickenham in the hope of seeing you again. I hope he isn't too angry. Why, my dear love, what's wrong?"

She felt as though she was going to faint and sat down bowing her head and he was beside her with his arm about her telling her to take her time and not to mind what she had to tell him.

"Let us not speak of Lord Orford but of ourselves," he said. "The Mediterranean ships are to sail immediately they are ready and I must go to Portsmouth tomorrow. Can you be ready to come with me?"

"Oh God! Do you go so soon? I'd hoped it might not be yet."

"This comes as a shock, even though you expected it. I know how such things are," he said comfortingly. "But you were pale when you came in. It's not one of your headaches?"

"No. I'm quite well—except my heart weighs a ton," she said.

"Because you'll be leaving Agnes and your father! That's natural, my dear. But you'll look forward to them joining us next year. Why, you'll be so busy you won't have time to miss them!"

"It isn't that, O'Hara. I don't know how to tell you."

"If you can't be ready tomorrow then let it be the next day. Or the next. We shan't sail at once. I have to be at Portsmouth, but you can follow in a day or two."

"I'd follow you to the ends of the earth. But I can't come. I simply can't come. O'Hara, I'm half killed with grief!" and she burst into a wild and passionate weeping.

He had never seen her in such distress and soothed her, holding her to his heart and stroking her dark hair and asking what was wrong, what had happened after she left him so bravely only yesterday?

"I didn't tell Lord Orford. He was too ill," she managed to say at last.

"He's always ill," O'Hara said.

"If I were to leave him now, so suddenly, it would kill him," she said. "My only wish is to be with you but it's impossible for the present. I haven't slept all night with the agony of making this decision."

"Do you mean you have decided already— alone—without consulting me?"

"I had to."

"And I am to go without you? Is that what you are telling me?"

"What else can be done?"

He drew away from her, got up and walked to the fireplace, leaning his head on the mantel. After an age he turned.

"You can tell me the truth," he said.

"Oh!" she gasped.

"Yes, Mary. The truth. I know you too well to be deceived. You are keeping something from me."

She gazed at him piteously and he crossed back, took her hands and looked steadily in her eyes. His voice was full of compassion.

"My dear love, I consider myself your husband already," he said. "There can be no secrets between husband and wife. Tell me honestly what troubles you. I shall be as silent as the grave. Trust me, Mary. Only trust me."

"I do trust you, but there's nothing else to add. We must give Lord Orford time to grow used to the idea of my leaving him."

"Hang it no! The time to tell him is the night before you leave your father's house to join me. Let him rail as he will—and he will rail, I've no doubt. He'll get over it and love you as much as ever."

"That would be most unwise. Old people can't stomach shocks and this has all been hasty. And there are many things at home I have to see to, things to be thought of and arranged . . ." she gabbled on with a string of threadbare excuses, but he was looking at her with an expression of distrust. He was not believing what she said.

"Believe me," she begged. "I am thinking of others, not of myself!"

"I believe that most sincerely. But you are still keeping something from me. Either you or— perhaps both of us—are being manipulated like puppets. Who's at the bottom of it? Lord Orford? Your father? Agnes?"

She shook her head. Oh, if only she could tell him! If only she could pour out the whole sordid story!

"Is it the Stick?" The question rapped out like a

pistol shot and she drew back in alarm.

"No!" she exclaimed. "Why do you suspect our best friend?"

"Because of her seditious ideas, her scorn of marriage and her mad notions of women's rights. What does she say in all those letters she writes you?"

"You may read them all. They're only full of plans for our future. Anne sees and understand my difficulties—she wishes our marriage with all her heart. Would she invite us to meet here if that were not so? You wrong her, O'Hara."

"Then confide in me—not in her. Tell me exactly what exists in this country strong enough to keep you from my side. I don't care what it may be. If it's anything discreditable—shameful—don't spare my feelings, or your own. Nothing can affect my love for you or my intention to marry you."

"There isn't anything I can say, except to beg you to try to understand that what I do now is done for others and the last person I'm considering is myself."

Her whole heart was in what she said: her white face and anxious eyes pictured the depths of her misery. His own face was pale and he looked uncertain what to do. Then he was at her feet smothering her hands with kisses, begging her to forsake all others and to be his wife.

"You think of others, never of yourself, I know. But do you think of me?"

"Continually. But I have a duty to those who depend on me and I shall fulfil it by staying a little longer—just as you will fulfil yours by going now. In a short time all my obligations will be discharged and then I shall be free to devote my whole life to you. May we not be even happier because of this delay?'' she asked eagerly.

"More sacrifices,'' he said. "They never bring joy. Be selfish, Mary. For once in your life, dearest Mary, I urge you to be selfish.''

She shook her head. "I should not be your dearest Mary if I were.''

"If my heart were beating in your breast you would pity me!''

"Must you hurt me more?'' she cried, letting caution go. "There are a hundred things weighing me down that I can't tell you, but if you could only know them you would have no doubts of me and of the misery I suffer. I love you with my heart and soul and body, but I can't leave home just now.''

"You say a hundred things oppress you? My dear, dear soul, I knew you were keeping a guard on your tongue. If I could manage to delay a few more days would you be free to tell then?''

"Never. You mustn't ask it,'' she said.

"When we are married?''

"Not even then. I shouldn't have said so much, but you stung me to it and I am wretched.''

It seemed a long time before he spoke. He was remote and withdrawn.

"If waiting a little will give you peace of mind I must submit to it although I scarcely know how,'' he said at last. "Oh Mary, you are the most adorable, irresistible creature in the whole of creation.''

He took the handkerchief she was clutching and

wiped her tears away so gently that she only wept the more and he began to talk optimistically as though he meant to smother his disappointment and frustration by dwelling on the future.

Her worst fears began to subside.

"I shall trust you to come to me as soon as you can," he said. "In the meantime you must write me long letters every day. Think about our house on the Rock and of our being there together with the Mediterranean sparkling away all around us."

"Oh, I shall conjure up such plans! And you'll reply?"

"Indeed I shall, though you'll be hard put to it to read my writing for my arm grows weaker."

"Then only write a little. O'Hara, dear O'Hara, you need me so!"

"If anything can cure me it will be your tenderness and solicitude," he said, and at this her soul cried out for freedom to go with him. He saw her stricken look.

"I shall mend as soon as I have you to coddle me," he said cheerfully, and he talked to the future with a confidence that dispelled her fears and made her almost happy again.

"You will never doubt me, will you? You will never trifle our happiness away?" she whispered.

He clasped her to his heart.

"I shall never love anyone but you," she said.

"And I shall be sustained by the knowledge that when we meet again it will be for life, Mary," he said.

He had never looked so fine, so noble, and his magnificent dark eyes glowed with ardour as he said again: "For life, my dearest Mary."

21

AND LIFE WENT BY.

The sea sparkled blue round the Rock of Gibraltar and the grey waves rolled up the English Channel. The young Corsican artillery officer who drove the English from Toulon in 1793, capturing General O'Hara among his prisoners, became Emperor of France and added conquest to conquest, but he had fallen and died in exile long since.

In England kings had reigned and died and now the youthful Queen Victoria was on the throne. So a lifetime had gone by.

One March evening a plump old clergyman called Sydney Smith crossed Hyde Park on his way to Curzon Street to call on the two Miss

Berrys and to ask if he might bring a new young man, a Mr. Charles Dickens, to dine with them one day.

He supposed there was bound to be a crowd as it was Mary's birthday and he realised with a start that she must be seventy-five. Absurd! She didn't look anything like.

Mary, sitting before her glass, was rather of the same opinion though she hadn't felt quite herself that day and had been half inclined to tell Harrot not to light the hall lamp. The moment their light showed all their friends, the statesmen, the writers, the wits and beaux who still flocked to see her, would start knocking at the door.

Sometimes she couldn't help thinking her drawing room was a little like the apartment of the maids of honour to the Princess of Wales which dear Lord Orford had been so fond of talking about. Only the maids of honour had been young and beautiful and she and Agnes were undoubtedly old.

She peered into the glass, smoothed on a little more rouge and a dab of pearl powder—what on earth would she look like without it—and turned with a smile as Agnes came in.

"Such a crowd already," Agnes said. "Are you coming down?"

"In a moment," Mary said, adjusting her lace cap.

Agnes looked at her rather anxiously. "Are you all right, Mary? You look a little triste," she said. "Nothing's upset you, has it?"

"Of course not," Mary said, hastily pushing

something to the back of a drawer. "I'm just a little fluttered, that's all."

She didn't want Agnes to know she had shed a few tears.

The buzz of voices came up from below. That was Sydney Smith. No mistaking his laugh.

"Dear Sydney—I do hope he's feeling better," she said.

"I think he must be—he just asked Harrot to grill him a butterfly's wing," Agnes said, preceding Mary downstairs.

From the hall Mary could see the room was already full enough for comfort and, noting her chosen women friends had been admitted, she said firmly: "Now, Harrot, no more petticoats. But you may admit one or two more men." And she gave the maid the names of those she wished to see.

With that she sailed into the drawing room, erect and graceful and pretty and with apparently effortless ease she created an atmosphere of relaxation in which conversation sparkled. She had the effect of champagne. Sydney Smith told everyone of his despair when she was ill and swore he'd commit suicide if she dared to die before he did. He'd dive out of the pulpit of St. Paul's.

People didn't stay too late—some of them thought she looked tired. Such nonsense! One young man amused her. When he took her hand he said he felt as though he was in direct contact with everyone he'd ever heard her speak of—with Walpole and Conway, Pope and Gay, Beau Brummel and Fox and all that brilliant Whig society.

It was fanciful but rather pleasant, though she had never met some he spoke of—only heard of them from dear Lord Orford who always made her feel as though she knew them. And from Lady Ailesbury and Mrs. Damer who had moved in such brilliant and exalted circles.

But she supposed young people would think that she moved in exalted circles, too. They always asked if she's actually seen Marie Antoinette. And spoken to Lord Byron? Indeed she had. And so many, many more whose names were almost legends.

"How strange I once prophesied I'd have a salon and everyone would flock to it," she thought. "I never dreamed it would be quite like this!"

Now they had all gone except the last comer, a tall and strikingly handsome young man with thick hair, beautiful dark eyes and such a strong sensitive face.

Her heart gave a dreadful little lurch when she looked at him. Surely it wasn't possible to feel so much emotion—after all this time? She ought to have told Harrot not to let him in.

But there he was before her, bowing over her hand with that exquisite courtliness she had never expected to see again, and he was thanking her for receiving him in a deep voice which was so like . . . so like . . .

She needed all her years of experience as a hostess in the social galaxy to preserve her composure and it stood her in good stead. She asked him to sit beside her and soon put him at his ease.

Of course he asked about Byron and about Sir Walter Scott who had often come to breakfast and stayed to read plays with her. And was it true she had written a play herself?

"Yes indeed, and what a dismal failure it was! It only ran for three nights at Drury Lane. I was mortified at the time. Fancy," she couldn't help a little chuckle, "people said it was most improper! Only think of that!"

But she had done quite a deal of literary work in her time and dear Sydney Smith had been such a help with some of it and had made her laugh so much into the bargain. Then of course she had travelled energetically, and met so many people. It would be easier to list those she hadn't than those she had!

"But you didn't come to hear of all these people, I think," she said at last. "You came because of . . ." her voice faltered but her eyes met his.

"Because of O'Hara," he said simply.

She laid her hand on his, too overcome to speak. That name had not been spoken aloud for many years although it was always in her mind.

"You are the only one who can tell me about him—the only one who really knows," the young man said.

"You—you never saw him?"

"When I was born he had been dead twenty years and my mother, his natural daughter, had nothing to tell me. She had no recollection of him. But his friend Mr. Barnes took an interest in me and it was he who spoke of you, and always with such admiration."

Memories, held at bay so long, flooded back.

She had been ill for a long time when O'Hara died seven years after they parted and through all the time of that separation she had hoped, secretly but fervently, that they would meet again.

"Please tell me," the young man said.

And Mary began. It was almost as though she was inspired as she recounted the whole story from her first meeting with O'Hara to the wonderful friendship that grew up between them and the love that came suddenly, miraculously, lighting up the world around her.

Her voice had a thrilling quality as she spoke and to her hearer it was the voice of a young woman and her face by the lamplight was young, too. And beautiful.

And as she spoke there was someone else in the room. Insubstantial perhaps, and yet more vital than either of them. The young man felt him, saw him, the magnificent, brave, wrong-headed, impetuous, valiant O'Hara who had begun to doubt she loved him when the seas rolled between them and had allowed this unfounded suspicion to fester in his mind until she was forced to realise with unutterable anguish that he had indeed trifled their happiness away by losing the faith she had fancied impregnable.

"I know now that many of our letters never arrived so questions we asked of each other went unanswered. In times of war these things are inevitable so that is when faith must never falter," she said.

She realised now that O'Hara could not have

received her vital message telling him that she had informed Lord Orford of their plans which he had heard with understanding and that all was arranged for her to join him.

"Those months of my engagement were the happiest of my life," she said. But before she could set out she discovered that his love for her had grown cold and his confidence had crumbled away leaving bitterness in his heart and ruining her hopes.

"If we could but have met again, if only for an hour, everything would have been put right," she said quietly. "I believe that with all my heart."

Earlier that day she had opened a packet of O'Hara's letters which she had treasured secretly for over forty years. Such wonderful letters as they were! So simple and straightforward and affectionate. There was no doubt he had loved her dearly and she had been his "dear soul, his Irresistible."

And he never married, even though he had mistresses and children. She did not censure him for that, it didn't alter her love for him, and she treasured his memory.

And that was why she allowed this young man who might so easily have been her own grandson if things had gone well, to call on his way through London, for he was going to be married and sail to America and a new life. She mustn't send him away thinking all this had been a tragedy! She had such splendid memories to give him and, for her own part, she had been quite successful in a way few single women had the fortune to be.

''I should have liked to marry but when I found I was to be solitary I decided I was not meant to be unhappy so I determined to be an agreeable woman of the world,'' she said.

''But you were so sought after! And now your salon is like those of the great French ladies, I hear. Miss Berry, dare I ask it? Did you ever fall in love again?''

Mary looked into his eyes and shook her head. Long ago O'Hara had taken her in his arms and said: ''When we meet again it will be for life.''

His voice still rang in her ears.

''There was never any man for me but O'Hara,'' she said. ''You see, in my heart, love is indelible.''

Don't Miss these Ace Romance Bestsellers!

_____ #75157 **SAVAGE SURRENDER** $1.95
The million-copy bestseller by Natasha Peters,
author of Dangerous Obsession.

_____ #29802 **GOLD MOUNTAIN** $1.95

_____ #88965 **WILD VALLEY** $1.95
Two vivid and exciting novels by
Phoenix Island author, Charlotte Paul.

_____ #80040 **TENDER TORMENT** $1.95
A sweeping romantic saga in the
Dangerous Obsession tradition.

74

The Novels of
Dorothy Eden
$1.75 each

07931	Bride by Candlelight
07977	Bridge of Fear
*08184	The Brooding Lake
*09257	Cat's Prey
*12354	Crow Hollow
*13884	The Daughters of Ardmore Hall
*14184	The Deadly Travelers
*14187	Death Is A Red Rose
*22543	Face Of An Angel
*47404	The Laughing Ghost
*48479	Listen To Danger
*57804	The Night of the Letter
*67854	The Pretty Ones
*76073	Shadow of a Witch
*76972	Sleep in the Woods
*77125	The Sleeping Bride
*86598	Voice of the Dolls
*88533	Whistle for the Crows
$94393	Yellow Is For Fear and Other Stories

Available wherever paperbacks are sold or use this coupon.

ace books, (Dept. MM) Box 576, Times Square Station
New York, N.Y. 10036
Please send me titles checked above.

I enclose $................. Add 35c handling fee per copy.

Name ....

Address ....

City.................... State............. Zip........

5H

There are a lot more
where this one came from!